# CUTS YOU UP

## DAVID BLACKWOOD

GHOST FOREST PRESS

Book Design by Truborn Design
www.truborndesign.com

For
Glenn Danzig
&
Peter Murphy

## PRELUDE: NIGHT THEY MISSED THE METAL SHOW

You should know, first of all, that I am an unreliable narrator. Of course I am. All first-person narratives are unreliable. People are unreliable. Human memory is unreliable. The cliche is that we see what we want to see, but it's not that. It's that we forget what we don't want to remember. And the things we do remember, we remember in our own way. We remember things the way we perceived them at the time. And when we remember them it's like playing an old record. Every time we take out those old memories and play them back, we put new scratches on them. And play them on different equipment, listen to them with different ears. So the song changes. And the song was only our interpretation to begin with. It may be flawed, but it's my song and I'm the only one who knows it. So I'll sing it my way.

We were hurtling down the street and Nick Cave was asking which one of us wanted to die. That's how I remember it, anyway. That's how I remember everything from that time. Intense and vivid. Even the boredom was intense. No mere malaise, but oppressive and crushing, like a thick fog that won't lift. Childhood in a small town in rural Virginia in the

Eighties was a mixture of the banal and the wondrous. Stultifying Sunday School lectures. The same Fourth of July parade every year, with the same old man driving his same Model T. The man getting older but the car never changing.

But the summer nights were gorgeous and fragrant, the air perfumed so heavily with honeysuckle and mimosa that the scent made you lightheaded. The cool shadowed woods where whitetails grazed indifferently and where you could eat yourself sick on blackberries. The autumn nights were woodsmoked and crisp and ghosts rustled through the dry maple and oak leaves. Fireflies danced in the graveyards and peep frogs sang you to sleep every night.

The times when I was with my friends seemed to sparkle with dark and vibrant colors. A delirious rush from one experience to the next. I've never felt that way since. Everything since that night has seemed blunted and distant, like I'm watching my life on a movie screen. That was the last night I was ever really happy.

One of the cruel ironies of life is that we seldom know when things are about to come to an end. We rarely see the change coming. If we did, would we pause and take in one of the last moments? Hold it in our memory like a snapshot to look back on later and say "that was when things were still good"? We spend most of our time worrying about things that will never happen and we're blind-sided by the things that actually change our lives. And it's only in retrospect that we appreciate those times before the change came.

Of course, we weren't actually "hurtling." I was driving my 1982 Volkswagen Rabbit, lovingly dubbed The Bunny of Death. Green paint faded to the color of pea soup, band stickers plastered over the rust spots. Bauhaus, The Cure, The Sisters of Mercy, and of course The Misfits' Fiend Club skull. There were dollar store Halloween decorations, skulls and witches, taped to the insides of the windows. A rubber bat dangled from the rearview mirror.

I had inherited the car from my older brother Alan when he joined the Navy, because it wasn't worth selling. That car wasn't capable of hurtling anywhere, unless one were to drive it off of a cliff. It sputtered and chugged and, if I had passengers, struggled to get up to highway speed. I was just happy if it didn't stall when I stopped at a traffic light. But it got me around, was a glimpse of freedom from our small town existence. And the tape player worked. Alan made sure of that. He might have had to push it off the road occasionally, wait for the engine to cool down before restarting it. But when he got it going again, he could listen to his music.

Music was always important in my family. My dad liked Johnny Cash and my mom was an Elvis fan. Alan was into skate punk. So, by the time I started discovering my own musical tastes, my parents fretted a little over the song titles and the dark imagery. But, they mostly accepted that it was my "thing" and that it was okay for them to not get it. Besides, after years of my older brother blasting The Circle Jerks from his stereo, there wasn't much that I could do that would shock them.

We were listening to "Sonny's Burning" by The Birthday Party, I'm sure of that. I had that song on a mixtape that I listened to constantly back then. It was early November 1990. We were on our way to a concert and we were all made up. I had just dyed my hair a few days before, because my natural brown was showing at the roots, and I wouldn't be seen at a concert with my hair any other color except black. I had it teased up like Robert Smith and I had done my makeup to try to look like Siouxsie Sioux. I'm sure it was a pale imitation, but at the time I thought it looked great. My skirt was long and flowing black. My mom called it my "gypsy witch skirt." My one pair of fishnets. And the black motorcycle boots that I stole out of Alan's closet. They were too big for me and I had to cinch the laces down tight, and even then they still gave me blisters for the first month. But they looked so cool. I had on my favorite shirt: Christian Death's "Only Theatre of Pain." I wish I still had that shirt. I tried to get it back from the cops afterward. They said I couldn't have it because it was evidence. Plus they cut it off of me at the hospital. And I guess it probably has a lot of blood on it. Still, it makes me sad to think of it sitting in an evidence locker. Or being incinerated, or whatever it is they do to evidence in closed cases.

Elise was in the passenger seat, her hair bleached almost white. Elise was older, wilder. If this were a movie, she would have been the sarcastic, sex-crazed best friend who my parents think is a bad influence and who shows her tits in the first half hour. In reality we were both sarcastic and we both took turns being a bad influence on each other. And while Elise was as interested or disinterested in sex as any other teenager, she was self-conscious and didn't even like showering in front of the other girls after gym. Elise liked some of my goth music, but her true love was still glam metal. Guns N Roses, Motley Crue, Skid Row. Anything dark and sexy and dangerous. She still wore acid-washed jeans, the knees ripped out. The same pair she had worn for the last two years, getting too small for her now. She wouldn't replace them, she said, because they were comfortable and she couldn't afford a new pair and if the tightness made the guys look at her butt a little more, then that was just a bonus. I always picture her wearing her Appetite For Destruction shirt. It was her favorite. But that's not right. She couldn't have been wearing that one, because that was the one they buried her in.

Joey was in the back. Probably stoned. He usually was, but I forbade him to smoke in my car. Pot, anyway. We were all smoking cloves because we thought it made us look exotic and sophisticated. Parents didn't make too much of a big deal about kids smoking cigarettes back then. They didn't like it, but figured it was better than other things we could be doing. It was a different time, I guess.

Joey was more of a metalhead, so he was wearing his Slayer shirt. He was chubby and quiet and had long stringy hair that he wore over his face like a mask. He didn't hang out with other metal fans, because they all called him a fag. He couldn't even wear his metal shirts at school, because he would get called a poseur. The jock and redneck metalheads didn't want to believe that a guy like him listened to the same music they did. He was shy and sensitive and got along better with girls. So, he hung out with us, even though he didn't like our music too much. He didn't really mind it, though, especially when he was stoned. We both loved Joey, but at the time we sort of thought of him as just being along for the ride. He went along with us on whatever adventures we would take him on. Quiet, passive, lost in a haze of pot smoke. Elise sometimes referred to him, behind his back, as our "pet boy." We vainly thought that he just hung around us because he had crushes on us. I know now that for someone to want to stay stoned all the time, they have to be trying to numb a lot of pain. We were dumb back then and we didn't think boys ever got sad, except when their football team lost. I used to think he was staring at my boobs all the time, but one day, looking back, it occurred to me that he never made eye contact with me. I'm not even sure if he liked girls. In retrospect, I think he was devoted to us simply because we were the first people who were ever really nice to him.

We had discovered Danzig the year before and they were the only band we all agreed on. Their music was dark and brooding enough to satisfy my goth tastes. It was metal enough for Joey. And it was dangerous and sexy enough for Elise. It told stories of forbidden things that fascinated us, that seemed genuinely dangerous. When we found out that they were playing in Richmond, a two hour drive away, the week after Halloween, we knew we had to go. But we never made it to the show. We never made it out of town.

I was driving, because I was the one with a car. That's just the way it was. I wasn't the leader or the Alpha or anything. I wasn't any prettier or smarter or more virtuous than any of my friends. So, I don't know why I was the only one who survived.

# 1

The line stretched clear across the store and for at least an hour it never seemed to get any shorter. Cassandra couldn't believe how many of them there were. She would have to admit to Anthony that he had been right and endure him playing "I told you so." He had been nagging her to do a book-signing for years. Insisting that her readers were clamoring for it. Her fans were devoted, sent her letters and emails telling her how much they loved the dark fantasy stories she wrote. Some sent drawings and paintings of her characters and a few had even gotten her words or cover art tattooed on their bodies. Their devotion was humbling.

But she was still skeptical that anyone would care about meeting her. She had always preferred to view her books as her only means of communication with the outside world. To her, the connection between an author and her readers was deeper and more meaningful than shaking hands and posing for pictures in a bookstore.

Now, however, her publisher was demanding it. Even making it a term of her new contract that she "actively participate in the promotion of the book." The landscape of publishing has changed, they said. Authors must have a "platform." Modern readers want to know the person who writes the books they read. Think of them as friends. Relate to them on a personal level. She would have to start regularly posting content to the social media accounts she had grudgingly started years before. She would have to do interviews. That was the reality. The days of the enigmatic literary recluse were in the past.

She was pleasantly surprised to see how many people were lined up just to have her scrawl her signature on their books. And they were all so polite and so shy. Some of them even seemed to be genuinely nervous to meet her. Cassandra found their sincerity and enthusiasm touching. After a while she even stopped being annoyed by the uncomfortable plastic chair the store had given her and the smell of carpet cleaner and the cloying easy listening music. The headache she was getting from the fluorescent lights refused to go away, though.

They were mostly young and almost all female. Lots of black clothing and heavy makeup. A few even dressed up as their interpretation of characters from her books. The elaborate effort they put into their appearances seemed almost absurd to her, and she was slightly embarrassed to remember the fashion excesses of her youth. Cassandra had given up on that kind of thing years ago. She barely wore any makeup now. Her hair was long and straight and she was secretly proud of the bits of gray that were beginning to appear. She wore a loose-fitting sweater and a long skirt. And the glasses- slightly tinted- that she never left the house without.

One by one, for hours, they came up to her table. Nervously, they put their books in front of her and awkwardly told her how much her work had meant to them. How much they were looking forward to reading the brand new copies of her latest book. And how many times they had read the well-worn copies of her earlier works. Some even asked her to sign the covers of their e-readers, which contained copies of all of her books. The whole thing seemed surreal.

Anthony was undoubtedly feeling smug. But, as always, he betrayed nothing. As stoic as ever, he stood by the table, scanning the crowd as they filed past him. He drew nervous glances from the fans. As the only black man in a room filled mostly with white women, it was hard for him to be inconspicuous. He was also 6'5" and broad-shouldered, so he drew attention wherever he went. He was dressed in one of his extensive collection of Brooks Brothers suits. A navy blue three-piece with a subtle, tasteful pinstripe. The suit was contrasted with a vivid red bow tie and matching silk pocket square. The suit and his round wire-frame glasses made him look like either the world's most sophisticated hitman or a pro football player turned accountant.

After several hours, the line was finally dwindling and the end was in sight. Cassandra was exhausted. She hadn't interacted with this many people in the previous five years combined. Her hand was beginning to cramp from all the signing, and her back was stiff from the uncomfortable chair. She barely looked up as a young woman in her early twenties approached the table and stood awkwardly looking at her. Many of them did this, waiting for Cassandra to be the first to say something.

"Hi, did you have something you want me to sign?"

She had an odd smile. A few of the fans Cassandra had signed for had that look. Not nervous like the others, but oddly excited. Like they were looking at some exotic animal in a zoo. The young woman nodded and pulled a worn paperback from her bag and slid it across the table.

"Will you sign this for me?" she asked.

Cassandra glanced at the cover quickly. She had seen it many times before, but not in years.

"That's not my book," she said. "It's bad form for a writer

to sign a book they didn't write." She tried to remain calm, like a Mother patiently explaining to her child that what they were doing was offensive. But Anthony could hear the tension rising in her voice, so he took a step closer to the table.

"But it is your book. It's about you." She was becoming insistent now.

Cassandra pushed the paperback a few inches away from her, touching it as little as possible. Anthony leaned over to look at the cover. The book was called "Bloodletting: The Dark Hollow Falls Massacre and the One Girl Who Survived." The cover was tabloid sensationalist, with the title in garish red and a grainy newspaper photo of a teenage Cassandra, covering her mouth in an expression of grief. Anthony was aware of the book's existence, of course, but he had never seen a copy of it.

"I know what it's about," Cassandra said. "And it most certainly is not about me. It's a work of fiction, that purports to be about something that happened to me. But as you can clearly see by the cover, it was not written by me. See, it says Persephone Ross right there. Feel free to have Ms. Ross sign her work of fiction. But it has nothing to do with me."

Cassandra was having trouble keeping the agitation from her voice, so Anthony leaned down to make sure that he was in the young woman's line of sight. Until then, she had been staring intently at Cassandra and didn't even seem to register his presence. He gently pushed the book back across the table to the young woman.

"Ma'am," he said and the young woman looked away from Cassandra for the first time. "If you have any of Ms. Watson's books, she will be happy to sign them. But, she will not be signing any other authors' work. Is that understood?" His tone was polite, but firm enough to make it clear that there was only one acceptable answer to his question.

The young woman took her book back and stammered,

"Look, I just thought...It's a famous case. That's what everyone knows you for. It's a part of history..." she was becoming indignant as she spoke, so Anthony cut her off, more forcefully this time.

"Ma'am" he said sharply. "There are people in line behind you who have books they would like to have signed. They have waited very patiently. Now, if you will excuse us, Ms. Watson can sign their books for them." His stare left no doubt that further discussion would be pointless.

"Have a lovely evening," he said as the young woman stomped out of the store. She muttered something as she was leaving, but the only word Anthony could make out was "bitch." He turned to address the remaining fans in line and thanked them for their patience.

The last few made their way through, one by one. She acknowledged each of them with a tired smile and polite thanks and was relieved when it was over.

# TRACK 1: A FOREST

Once, three friends went out on a chilly November night. They were on their way to a grand ball. And they asked for the moon to give them light, for they had many a mile to go that night. They traveled through the forest and the grass was coated with frost. And it glistened like diamonds and it crunched beneath their feet like bones.

Cassandra was beautiful but melancholy. Her hair was like spun ebony. Her skin was as fair as fresh linen. Her lips the color of crushed summer blackberries. Her friend Elise was bold and reckless, but wise. With hair like polished platinum and eyes the color of the sky reflecting off of Arctic ice. Joey was a boy not handsome nor brave, but he was loyal and pure of heart.

Along their way, they stopped to rest in an old abandoned house by the graveyard. They had been in this house many times before. As small children, they would sneak in to prove their bravery. And when they were older, it became their secret hiding place. But they had never been there so late at night. Would there be ghosts walking the halls by moonlight? Would dreadful crones stir cauldrons bubbling with the flesh of unbaptized children in the basement?

They were frightened, but they didn't meet any monsters. Not yet.

But later that night, after losing their way in the forest, they did meet a monster. And he was more horrible than any ghost or witch they could have imagined. And they were lured into his lair where they saw the blood and bones of the children he had lured there before.

And only one of the friends escaped, because she was brave and beautiful and virtuous.

And the others were baked into bread.
    And their hearts were buried in a glass casket.
    And a trail of their blood on the white road led the way to the monster's lair.
    And vines twisted through their ribcages and blood-red roses bloomed there every November.
    And a juniper tree grew on the spot where they were killed.
    And the little ones chewed on their bones-o....

# 2

Back in her hotel room, Cassandra slumped into an armchair by the window. The lights were dimmed, so she had taken off her tinted glasses. Bright lights made her left eye burn and water. Anthony had taken off his suit jacket and hung it neatly on a coat hanger, even though he knew he wouldn't be staying long. He sat on the edge of the bed and made sure the creases in his pants were straight.

"How are you feeling?" he asked.

"Exhausted."

"But you're okay? No aches or pains? I know that was a long time for you to be sitting in one position. And that chair didn't look very comfortable."

"I'm fine. I would tell you if I wasn't." She looked absently out the window at the building across the street. Another hotel probably.

He tried to lighten the mood a little. "So, that wasn't too bad, now was it?"

She shook her head. "Can you believe someone brought that garbage and asked me to sign it? Who in their right mind would think that was okay?"

He shrugged. "Kids. Raised by the Internet. They don't

think of public figures as actual people. Some of them don't seem to think of anyone but themselves as actual people. But, leaving aside the one bad apple, it wasn't as bad as you thought it would be, was it?"

"No. It was fine. And all the rest of them were very nice."

"Good. Because you have six more of these to do. And we have an early flight tomorrow. And don't forget that once we arrive in New York, you have an interview with that young lady from the Times."

She groaned. Interviews were another annoyance imposed on her by her publisher's contract.

"Why can't I just do it by e-mail? E-mail interviews are so much easier."

"Well, yes they are. And e-mail interviews are fine for the smaller, genre publications. But, the New York Times Review of Books insists on face-to-face interviews."

"But I am a genre writer. I write fantasy."

"Now now, my dear. No false modesty, please. Alas, you have won numerous literary awards. Therefore, you are a literary writer. And if you would like to maintain your status as one, and as a New York Times bestseller, and to continue to stay in the good graces of booksellers, you have to play the game. That's just how it works."

He chuckled nervously. She glared at him.

"I know that chuckle. That's the innocent little boy chuckle that you always give me when you're about to tell me something that's going to annoy me."

"Well, I was going to wait until we were in New York to tell you this, but I suppose this is as good a time as any. On Wednesday you're scheduled to tape an interview for The Daniel DiSilva Show."

"A television interview?"

"Yes. Television. That's where shows are shown."

"Don't be flippant. You know I don't do television."

"I know, I know. But we don't really have much choice in the matter. Your editor feels that you are poised for a mainstream breakthrough, and DiSilva has a lot of pull with mainstream book buyers. It will be less than an hour and then it will be over. And don't worry, I've given them strict instructions on what he can and cannot ask you."

"God, DiSilva is such a pompous jackass though."

"Yes, but unfortunately, he's a pompous jackass with a lot of influence."

She got up stiffly from her chair. In a small room with solid, reassuring objects to place her hands on she walked confidently. Even without the cane, she showed little difficulty getting around. She retrieved her water bottle from the mini fridge and sat on the bed, propped against the pillows.

"Fuck. I swear once this is over, I'm never writing another book again."

"Fine, fine. You can just get a job waiting tables. And I'll find some other young literary ingenue to take under my wing."

Cassandra sat and stewed for a few minutes.

"Any other surprises you were planning to spring on me?"

"No." He rubbed the back of his neck. "However, I suppose we might as well have 'The Talk' now."

"Oh? And what talk would that be? If it's the one about where babies come from, I already know all about that."

"No," he said patiently. "It's the talk that we have once a year or so."

"You mean, the one about how I should think about going out on dates, socializing more, 'engaging with the rest of the human race'?"

"No," he said." I mean the one about your future financial security. And choices you can make now that would make life easier for you down the road."

Cassandra resented having to discuss money. As far as she

was concerned, she paid Anthony so she wouldn't have to think about money.

"I hired the financial planner that you recommended. I'm investing as much as I can in whatever he suggests."

"Which is all well and good. But you could be making a lot more money than you are. As your manager, I feel I would be remiss in my duties if I didn't advocate courses of action that would be more profitable."

"And what 'courses of action' did you have in mind?"

He was still sitting on the edge of the bed, still looking forward at the place she had been sitting. He turned to look at her now.

"Well. One that you might consider is writing the book that publishers have been asking you to write for twenty years."

"Oh, I see!" She looked skyward in mock revelation and then back down at him. "This is the talk where you try to get me to dredge up the worst experience of my life and exploit it for profit. That's the book you're talking about, right? The one about the time I watched my two best friends get brutally murdered?"

He turned back and looked out the window again.

"Yes. And yes, it would be very profitable. But, wouldn't it also be... cathartic? You're an artist and artists channel their pain into their works."

"Oh, is that what we do?"

He got up and started pacing.

"Sylvia Plath would have written about it."

"Oh yeah, and look how well things turned out for her. Sadly, I can't follow in her footsteps. My oven is electric."

"Okay, okay. Bad example." He thought for a moment. "Joyce Carol Oates would write about it."

"Yes, that's true. Joyce Carol Oates would write a novel about her car breaking down. And it would be wonderful. The most moving novel ever written about a car breaking down. It would probably win a Pulitzer. But, I'm not Joyce Carol Oates."

"No, you're not. But what you are is forty-five years old. And you don't really have a retirement fund. And you don't have health insurance. And your medications keep getting more expensive. Healthcare costs are only projected to rise in the next ten years."

"Well, Christ, if it's that bad, maybe I should just follow Sylvia's example."

"Honey, no." He sat next to her on the bed and wanted to put his hand on her shoulder. But he stopped himself, knowing that touching her when she was upset only made it much worse. "I'm not telling you all of this to upset you. I know you don't like thinking about these things. That's why you hired me. To worry about it for you. And that's what I'm doing. I'm worrying about it."

She slouched down on the pillows and stared at the ceiling.

"Do I need more money? Why can't we just sell the movie rights to something?"

"We've already optioned every book you've written. Until someone actually decides to make one into a movie, we don't get any more money. It could happen tomorrow. All of these new streaming services are looking for books to turn into movies. But your books, I'm sorry to say, are just odd enough and dark enough to make movie studios nervous. But, part of the reason we're doing all of these interviews and signings and other dreadful things, is in the hope that they will kindle enough public interest to make a studio take a chance on one of them. Society is changing and people are open to things they never would have accepted ten years ago. But, I like to keep our options open. And writing something... autobiographical would open up a lot more options."

"Am I running out of money?" He could tell she was getting exasperated.

"No, no. Not at all. You should be fine for at least another year. But, I like to think long term. And I like to know how I'm going to handle a problem, before the problem manifests itself. It's the Marine in me. 'If you fail to plan, you plan to fail.'"

They sat for a few moments in silence. Then she rose from the bed, her stiff strained movements betraying her earlier assertion that she wasn't in pain. "I need a drink."

"I'm sorry," he said. "I really didn't want to upset you."

"It's fine," she poured herself some vodka into one of the hotel's water glasses. "You're just doing your job."

"We should get some sleep. I'll call you around... six?"

"Fine."

He got up and retrieved his jacket from its hanger. His room was next door, but he didn't like carrying his jacket folded over his arm. So he put it on, buttoning only one button. At the door, he stopped and turned around to her. "You know I love you, right?"

"Sure." She said, sipping her drink and staring out the window.

# 3

The set of "One For The Books with Daniel DiSilva" was a mock-up of a library with fake books on fake shelves. Cassandra sat in a fake leather armchair for what seemed like an hour, while technicians adjusted lights and makeup artists came by periodically to wipe off the sweat that kept accumulating on her brow. She shaded her eyes from the bright spotlight shining on her. DiSilva was nowhere to be seen.

Anthony was busy off set, quietly berating the producers. "Why the hell are those lights so bright? I told you they have to be dimmer. Her eye is very sensitive."

"We'll turn them down a little. But people have to be able to see her, for Christ sake."

"And where the hell is DiSilva? Is he going to grace us with his presence at some point?"

"He doesn't come on set until right before we start filming. He says it keeps things 'spontaneous.'"

The lights finally dimmed a bit more. Anthony walked onto the set and knelt beside Cassandra's chair. "Is that better? How's your eye?"

"I'm fine," she said with a sigh. "Can we just get this over with? Where the fuck is he?"

"I don't know. But, if he doesn't show up soon, I'm gonna go find him and drag his happy ass down here myself. I told them we had to be out of here by one o'clock."

"And what time is it now?"

"Almost noon."

Cassandra slumped in her chair a little. "So, we have at least another hour?"

A producer off set asked her to please sit back up, or they would have to adjust the lights again. Anthony tensed and was preparing to turn on the producer and tear into him, but a booming voice interrupted him.

"Morning, kids! Are we ready to do this?" DiSilva strode into the studio, patting backs and clasping upper arms. He was in shirtsleeves, and his salt and pepper hair was tousled in a way that he thought made him look boyish. He was immediately swarmed by makeup people who put touchups on his face and made his hair slightly less tousled.

"Why the fuck is it so dark in here?" DiSilva asked no one in particular. "What, are we filming a horror movie or something?"

The producer closest to him said something Cassandra couldn't hear. But they both looked in her direction, so she assumed it was about her. DiSilva nodded impatiently. "Fine. Whatever. It'll make the interview seem more intimate, I guess."

A production assistant appeared with DiSilva's jacket and helped him into it. Anthony approached him as he was buttoning up. "May I have a quick word?" he asked.

"Well, this isn't really the best time. Not sure if you noticed, but we're filming a TV show here."

"Yes," Anthony said. "I appreciate that. I've sent you several e-mails over the last week. Had you responded to any of them, we could have set up a better time for this discussion."

"Yeah? I'm sorry, but who are you again?"

"Anthony Lucas."

"Right, right. And you're what?" DiSilva paused to look Anthony up and down. "Her bodyguard or something?"

Anthony grinned. "No. I'm her manager. I take care of her affairs. Make sure that she is being treated properly. Although, if I were called upon to protect her physically, I am capable of that as well."

"No doubt," DiSilva said. "Were you a Marine, by any chance?"

"I *am* a Marine," Anthony replied. "Once a Marine, always a Marine. Why do you ask?"

"I could just tell. I was in the Navy, myself. *Was*. Once I got out, I was out. Anyway, I apologize. My email backlog is out of control lately. What was it you wanted to talk to me about?"

"The substance of this interview…"

"Right, right. We got your notes. My producers briefed me. Don't worry, I've been doing this interviewing thing for quite a few years. I know what I'm doing." He gave Anthony a quick pat on the shoulder and walked past him onto the set. He greeted Cassandra with a beaming smile that made her think he was about to ask her to vote for him or try to sell her a car.

"Cassandra. So nice to see you again." He took her hand in both of his and shook it. "I believe I interviewed you once before. It must have been, what, fifteen years ago? I believe it was at the National Book Fair in D.C., correct?"

"Wow." She was genuinely surprised. "You have a really good memory."

"Well," he said as he sat in his own fake leather armchair. "I never forget an interview. And I have a very good staff, who jog my memory if necessary. I certainly hope the long wait isn't an indication of how much you enjoyed our previous meeting." He gave a casual chuckle that was probably meant to be self-deprecating.

"No, no. Nothing personal. I just don't do many interviews. I prefer to let my work speak for itself."

"And it speaks loud and clear. Hey, that's not bad, we should reuse that exchange when we're actually filming. Speaking of which." He trailed off with a gesture of impatience to the director.

THE THEME MUSIC FADES IN, a Mozart piano concerto. The show logo fades onto the screen and then slowly fades out. The camera zooms slowly in towards DiSilva. He has his glasses on and is looking down at a book. As the camera settles in on his face, he looks up and removes his glasses. (Cassandra is amused to note that he carelessly drops the glasses onto the floor out of the camera's view.)

"Welcome to 'One For The Books with Daniel DiSilva.' I am your host Daniel DiSilva. And today we are pleased to welcome one of America's finest writers of contemporary fantasy, Cassandra Watson. She is the best-selling author of twelve novels and the recipient of numerous awards, including the World Fantasy Award and The Shirley Jackson Award. Her books have made four appearances on the New York Times Notable Books list. Her latest, 'It Calls Like a Distant Wind' is out now from Sutton House and is available in Hardcover, Audiobook, and ebook wherever books are sold. Cassandra, thanks for being here."

"Thank you for having me."

"Now, I believe I interviewed you once before, at The National Book Festival in Washington D.C. That must have been in 2003. I certainly hope that the long wait between interviews isn't a reflection of your feelings about the previous interview." He once again gave the same little chuckle.

"No, nothing personal. I just don't do many interviews." Cassandra found herself giving a casual chuckle as well. For a moment, she almost forgot to finish the phrase she was repeating. "I prefer to let my books speak for themselves."

"And they speak loud and clear. All the same, we're very happy to have a chance to speak with the mind behind those books. Now, you've been writing for almost two decades and your books have attracted a loyal following. Your stories have been described as 'mythic' and as 'modern day fables.' Joyce Carol Oates has called you 'the American Angela Carter.' How do you feel when you hear these descriptions?"

"Well, Joyce is very kind. And it's flattering, of course. Carter's work was profoundly influential, when I discovered it in my late teens. I had always been enamored of fables and fairy tales, and what I felt was their primal insight into human nature. Angela Carter showed me that those truths could be expressed in a way that was relevant to modern life. And that they weren't archaic and that Female Agency and sexuality didn't have to be bowdlerized out of them."

"Now, obviously, the social climate and the publishing world have changed dramatically since you started your writing career. Have you felt the effect of those changes? Do you think your books will still be relevant to a Millennial readership?"

"I'm not really sure what that means, honestly. As I said, the things I write about are universal and fundamental to the human experience. Human wants and desires and fears are the same now as they were in Aesop's time. I'm not aware of any fundamental change to basic human nature in the last decade."

"Of course not. However, there has been a shift in the social climate. Some Conservatives have criticized the violent and sexual imagery of your books. Others have accused you of sexualizing pubescent characters. And some Feminists have accused you of fetishizing violence against women."

"My books aren't for everyone, certainly. They delve into some of the darker aspects of the human mind. Some Feminists have a limited view of what is acceptable for Women to talk about and some of them want to keep Women's sexuality in a safe little box. Violence is a reality of life. My books are about how people deal with that reality and the effects of it. And real people don't always deal with these things in a socially acceptable way. Real people's sexuality is often messy. Especially in those who have been victimized. Most of my readers are women and I've received many letters from women who were victims of violence and who have told me that my books have helped them get over their feelings of shame and self-loathing."

"Would you say that violence fascinates you?"

"I suppose."

"Why, though?"

"Why? I don't know. Why is Cormac McCarthy fascinated with violence? Why was Jack London fascinated by the sea and wolves? Why was Anais Nin fascinated by sex? These are aspects of life. I've never understood the belief that artists should ignore certain aspects of life because some people find them distasteful. An artist's only obligation is to be honest."

"But, obviously, you don't write equally about all aspects of life. You don't write about going to the grocery store. Or shopping for life insurance."

"Well, I'm not John Updike. Some people have the talent for making the ordinary interesting. Others are called to portray the extremes. What was it Flannery O'Connor said? 'For the deaf, you shout. For the near-sighted, you draw violent images.' Something like that."

"Well, O'Connor was talking about gaining the attention of an audience that was hostile to your beliefs. That it was necessary to shout to get their attention and to get them to see the world the way you see it. Do you feel that is what you are doing?"

"I don't know." She was getting agitated and Anthony was pacing off set. He was surprised by how well she was handling herself, even though DiSilva was clearly disregarding the notes he had sent about what kind of questions were acceptable. She sat and collected her thoughts before responding. "I'm writing, not for an audience that is hostile to my beliefs, but for an audience that has been desensitized and taught to not feel unpleasant emotions. The modern reader is hostile to the idea that bad things are a part of life. They've been taught to believe that they deserve to have only good things happen to them. And they don't know how to deal with it when bad things inevitably come."

"Well, let's talk about that a little. You have of course had bad things happen to you in your life."

"As has everyone."

"Yes, but yours go a bit beyond the ordinary, don't they? You were famously the victim of terrible violence as a teenager. I'd like to talk about how that experience has affected your work."

Anthony grabbed one of the producers by a sleeve. "The fuck is he doing? He knows he's not supposed to ask about this!"

The producer gave him a helpless shrug. "He does what he wants. He gets good ratings for a show where people sit and talk about books. So, he has free rein. The network is afraid to piss him off."

"He doesn't want to piss me off. You get me? So, either he changes to a different topic, or this interview is over."

The producer simply responded with the same helpless shrug.

Cassandra sat, shaking her head. "I don't talk about that."

DiSilva wouldn't let it go. "You said that your obligation as an artist is honesty. And that your job is to confront the negative aspects of life. So where is that honesty when it comes to the negative in your own life?"

"In my art. In my books. It's all there for anyone who wants to read it. For anyone who wants to smell the blood and see all of my scars. But, I don't think I'm under any obligation to exploit my personal life to help you get ratings."

"You can't keep the world at arm's length forever. That's the real question: are you using your fiction to let people inside your head or to keep them out?"

Cassandra shook her head and gave a short, cynical laugh. Anthony said her name quietly from off set. She looked over to him and then back to DiSilva.

"You want to know what happens when you let people inside your head? Back in the early days of the Internet I used to print my email address in the backs of my books, so anyone could write to me. It was great, mostly. I got a lot of messages from shy readers telling how much my books meant to them. Asking me questions about my characters. Wanting to know how the next book was coming along.

"But, then one day I got an email that said that the sender had found some pictures that they thought I would like. It had a link to a photo gallery page. A lot of my fans do artwork based on my books and some of them had sent me links before. So I thought nothing of it. I clicked on the link and it took me to a 'true crime' website. The gallery was all pictures of..."

She stopped and clenched her fists. She took several deep breaths before continuing.

"... they were pictures of my friends. Crime scene photos. Autopsy pictures. My best friends in the world, cut up like animals in a slaughterhouse. This person, this stranger, wanted me to see those pictures. He sought me out. Found my email address, just so he could make me look at that. I don't know, got some kind of thrill out of knowing that he could hurt me with no risk to himself. Or maybe he didn't even put that much thought into it. Maybe he laughed about it for a few minutes and then forgot about the whole thing."

DiSilva was shaking his head with a pained look on his face. Cassandra thought that he probably practiced it in front of his mirror. "I'm sorry..." he started to say.

"I came pretty close to killing myself that night. I remember thinking about how much I wanted to be with my friends again. And thinking that it was ridiculous that I had fought so hard to survive. Because, who the hell would want to live in a world like this one?"

Cassandra looked over at Anthony. He was watching her intently. She began to take the wireless microphone off of her sweater and get out of her chair. DiSilva got up and tried to stop her. "What are you doing? We have about ten more minutes of show to fill."

Anthony was on the set in a few steps, putting himself between DiSilva and Cassandra. "She's leaving. You were told that she doesn't discuss this matter. Now, I would suggest that you sit down and let the lady be on her way."

DiSilva put his hands up and sat back down. "Okay. Okay."

As they walked out of the studio, the producer briefly thought about trying to stop them and convince them that the interview could be salvaged, but Anthony gave him a look that made him give it up as pointless. Just before Anthony closed the studio door behind him, he heard DiSilva saying "hey, thanks for wasting my afternoon." He hoped Cassandra hadn't heard it.

# TRACK 2: THE KILLING MOON

I remember the moonlight and the streetlights reflecting on broken glass. And it glittered like diamonds. And it glistened like ice. And the blood. The blood. Blood everywhere. And the streetlights, those blue-white streetlights, they made the blood look black. We bled black. We bled darkness. Haha, funny joke. We used to joke that we had black blood and black hearts, but I guess we were right, because our black blood was everywhere. I couldn't tell which blood was mine and which was hers. It didn't matter, though. We were blood sisters already. We cut our fingers and pressed the wounds together years before. Our first kiss. We bled into each other, and her blood was my blood.

I couldn't tell where I was bleeding from. I hurt in so many places that they all blended into each other until my whole body was one big open wound. Elise was bleeding worse, though. I know that. I'm not sure if I knew that then, but I know it now.

We were hiding. Hide and seek. Close your eyes and count to ten. It was like one of our sleepovers when we were younger. Tell me a ghost story. Tell me a scary story. I laughed. God help me, I actually laughed. How about this one right now? Is this story scary enough? Will stories ever scare me again? What's the worst thing that ever happened to you? Boy, have I got a story for you.

She started singing. She was singing when she... [I stopped here. I haven't cried in years, but I started crying when I typed this.] Elise was singing when she died.

*We were walking down the path, through the forest of snow. I led her by the hand, my bleeding hand in hers. The wound in my hand from when I shattered the glass casket she was imprisoned in. The sorcerer's curse, that only by wounding myself and wearing the scar forever, could I break and set her free. My blood ran through our interlaced fingers and drip-drip-dropped into the snow. It will leave a trail, I thought. A trail we can follow home if we get lost. The trees looked like elegant ladies, wrapped in their ermine coats of snow. And all around was a mysterious luminescence, the color of amethyst. We could see our way, but the luminescence tinted the blood droplets a rich purple-black on the white snow path.*

*We had to find the palace of The Ice Queen. For only she could save Elise. For when I broke her out of the casket, she showed no gratitude or relief or happiness. I soon found that she was incapable of showing any emotion at all. And when I ripped open her bodice, I discovered why. There in her chest was a cruel and ragged wound. I caressed it gently and spread it open, and I saw that her heart had been cut out and replaced with a lump of ice. Only the Ice Queen would be able to make her heart flesh again...*

She started singing and I couldn't tell what song it was. She was delirious. She wouldn't respond to me. Her eyes stared through me. That was when I knew how bad it was. I held her in my arms and she was cold and shaking. Her voice was barely a whisper, and she sang. I put my ear to her lips so I could hear what she was singing. I could finally make it out: "... we're in luck. If it rains all week, just pretend you're a duck. Quack, quack. Waddle, waddle..." And then she stopped.

I was so relieved that Elise's mother never asked me about her last moments. I don't know how I could ever tell her that her daughter's last words were "Quack, quack. Waddle, waddle."

# 4

The lights were out and she lay on her bed in the hotel room. The blanket was drawn up around her ears, but she could still hear every noise outside her room. Every laughing couple walking past in the hall seemed to be mocking her. Every door closing was like a gunshot. And where the Hell was Anthony? When she needed him? She burrowed further into her blankets and thought, for the thousandth time, that she was alone, in a city of millions, thousands of miles from home. Her eyes stung from crying, but she was too exhausted to cry anymore. She prayed to whoever might be listening that maybe sleep would overtake her soon. But her pounding heart and racing mind and jittering nerves made that an impossibility. She tried to control her breathing. Tried to remember some bit of advice that one of the therapists or meditation gurus had given her over the years, that might be of some use. All of it seemed like a pathetic joke now. Bandages that people had tried to slap over a cancer that grew year after year.

She must have dozed for a few minutes, through sheer exhaustion, because she woke with a start when Anthony finally came into her room and crouched by the bed and gently said "Cass.." She grabbed onto him as though she were drowning at sea and he was a life-boat.

"Goddamnit! Where were you? You were gone so long!" Her voice broke. "I thought you left me."

"I'm sorry, sweetie." He stroked her hair and she let him. That meant it was really bad. Physical contact usually made things worse when she was upset. For her to allow it, even initiate it, meant that she was absolutely terrified. Anthony had only seen her like that a few times before, and those had been years ago. "You know I wouldn't leave you."

"I don't know. I don't know anything."

"I'll never leave you. As long as your checks don't bounce." She laughed. But only a little.

"However," Anthony went on. "I had some business to take care of. Damage control."

"You didn't punch anyone, did you?"

"No. It didn't come to that."

"I mean, if you had punched DiSilva, I wouldn't be mad. I just don't want you to get arrested or sued."

"No, no. Nothing like that. I did have some choice words for him though."

Cassandra sat up in the bed and brushed the hair out of her face. "I can't do this anymore. You know that, right?" Anthony nodded. "I just need to go home. Sutton House can sue me. I don't care. I don't care if my career is over. I have things I can sell if I need money. And I thought of some other jobs I can do. I can type. I'm pretty fast, so I can do transcriptions. Some kind of work from home thing. I don't know. I'll sell my house if I have to. Live in an apartment. I guess I won't be able to pay you anymore though."

"I'm glad to see you thinking ahead. But, let's not start apartment-hunting just yet. As I said, I've been doing damage control."

"Did you convince DiSilva not to run the interview?"

"What, run from a fight? Moi? Surely, you know me better than that by now, darling."

"Oh god," she buried her face in her hands. "I just want this to go away. I don't want to talk about this anymore."

"Well, unfortunately, that's not really an option. At least not anymore. You can't just make things go away in the Internet age. Have you heard of The Streisand Effect?"

"Streisand? As in Barbra? What does everyone's mom's favorite singer have to do with this?"

"Well, my moms is more partial to Aretha. But, anyway... yes, Barbra. She once filed a lawsuit to keep the paparazzi from flying over her house and taking pictures. The lawsuit got so much publicity that even more pictures were taken and even more got published. In the modern media age, the more you try to hide something, the more coverage it gets."

"So, I'm screwed and we're back to me not writing anymore. I can not keep having the worst experience of my life dredged up again and again."

"No, we just have to accept that the questions are going to come. We have to meet them head-on and we have to be proactive about this. Which is what I should have done to begin with. I should have known that this would happen and I could have defused the situation from the start. I didn't and I regret that. But now I'm taking control of the situation. Take our friend DiSilva, for example. I let him have control of that interview. But I've taken the control out of his hands."

"Meaning what?"

"I took the liberty of releasing a statement on your Facebook page. The story is going to come out, so it's important that we are the first to announce it. I won't bore you with the entire text, but the gist is that DiSilva blindsided you, asked you questions about things you aren't comfortable talking about, tried to exploit your personal tragedy for ratings. I also called in a favor from my friend, Maria Oshiro. We've known each other since college and she is now a very well-respected literary blogger. She's a fan of your work, but she's never written about you before, because of our personal connection. And I would never dream of asking her to. But, I felt it necessary to call in the big guns, so to speak. She made a blog post, based on 'an anonymous tip' blasting DiSilva for exploiting you and trying to re-victimize you and for being insensitive to violence against women and....PTSD."

Cassandra groaned, rolled over, and buried her face in her pillow.

"And yes," Anthony continued. "I know you don't want people to think of you as a victim. Or the poster girl for violence survivors. But, unfortunately, this our best option right now."

"Goddamit! I don't want fucking sympathy!"

"I know that. But, you have to understand, society has changed in the last decade. We're lucky in a way. If this had happened ten years ago, the media would have crucified you and made you look crazy. But, people don't stand for that anymore. There is a lot more sensitivity to people...in your situation. The public attitude towards women who have been victimized has changed dramatically. People are on your side. Maria's blog post has already blown up in the last two hours. There is even a hashtag... remember when I explained hash-tags to you? Well, the hashtag #ISTANDWITHCASSANDRA is starting to trend."

Cassandra chuckled and shook her head. "This is insane. This all insane."

"And, best of all, I've got Sutton House on our side. George Sutton himself is going to release a statement of support in the morning. I don't know the exact verbiage, but they want it known that they stand behind you and that your well-being is their first priority."

"Sutton isn't pissed off that I'm canceling the rest of the tour?"

"Oh, of course he's pissed off. But admitting that publicly would make him look like the bad guy." Just then Anthony's phone rang, and he excused himself to take the call in the living room of the suite. Cassandra could hear his muffled voice through the door, but couldn't make out any words. She thought to herself: so this is what life is going to be like now. They'll never let me forget. I'm not a writer anymore, I'm just "that girl whose friends were killed."

Anthony had stopped talking on his phone and gently pushed the bedroom door open. "That was Howard, one of DiSilva's producers. I had been waiting to hear back from him."

"Please tell me he was calling to tell you that they're not running the interview."

"No. And we don't want that, remember? Streisand? We want people to see the way he treated you. It only makes him look bad and you look good."

"But how can they run the interview? I walked out when it was half over."

"That's what Howard and his staff have been working on. DiSilva has recorded an introduction for the interview. A big sappy mea culpa. He'll look all pained and abashed and apologize for his insensitivity and thank you for teaching him an important lesson about respect and yadda yadda yadda. I'm sure he doesn't believe a word of it, but it's his only way to save face at this point."

Cassandra shook her head in disbelief. "You did all of that while I was laying here?"

"Yes, ma'am." Anthony said, like a young boy waiting for his mother to tell him he did a good job. He might have even blushed a little.

"Amazing." She was still shaking her head. She almost smiled.

"See," he said. "That's why you gotta keep making sure those checks don't bounce. I've booked us a flight home at 8:00 AM. So, you need to get some sleep. Here." He pulled a pill bottle from his pocket and shook out a Xanax. "I know you haven't taken any in a long time, but I think it's called for." She took the pill and swallowed it with a gulp of water. Then, out of habit, she opened her mouth wide to show that it was empty.

"Good. You should take a shower, too. It'll help you relax. I'll sleep on the couch in the living room. So if you need me I'll be right outside your door, okay?" She nodded her head and dutifully trudged into the bathroom. She stripped down by the bathtub, turned on the hot water, took off her leg brace and sat down to pee as the bathroom filled with steam. When she was done, she turned the knob to make the water cooler and went to the sink and regarded herself in the mirror.

At home, there were no mirrors in her bathroom. Angela Carter had said "mirrors make a room uncosy" in one of her stories. Cassandra had banished them from her bathroom for the simple reason that sometimes she didn't like to see herself in the nude. Most of the time she would dress in the bathroom and then look at herself in the mirror in her closet. She did little with her hair and hadn't worn makeup in years, so these inspections were cursory at best. Note the gradual graying of the hair, the wrinkling of the face. She had once gone for almost two years without seeing her unclothed body, even showering by the soft dim illumination of candles. From time to time, though, she would make an examination. There were times when she felt disconnected from her physical form and had to look at herself and convince herself that yes, this is actually my body that I see.

She stood in front of the sink, lit by the bright vanity lights, and she ran her hands over her body. Her right breast was soft and beginning to wrinkle, to hang lower, and the nipple had darkened. Her left breast was truncated, swelling from her chest in the normal way but ending abruptly in a crescent scar that blended in to the skin above her ribcage. It had no nipple and resembled an elbow as much as it did a breast. At one time she had laughed at the irony that teenage boys would have once gone to great lengths to see that nipple. But what was left of it had been sliced off in an operating room and thrown into an incinerator. The other pieces probably lying on the ground in the woods somewhere. "There ya go, boys. Go out and find it and ogle 'til your heart's content".

She barely thought about these things anymore. No one aside from doctors and nurses had seen her naked in over twenty-five years. Her mother had tried to help her dress and undress and bathe the first few times. But she had broken down and started to sob each time, so Cassandra stopped asking for help and learned to do it on her own.

Below her ribcage was the neat orderly vertical scar, the "railroad track" as she thought of it, from the surgeon's main incision. It divided her torso from sternum to navel. On either side were the smaller scattered marks and, if she thought about it, she could remember how she had gotten each one. A knife here, a piece of broken glass there. The long diagonal slashes on her hip and side from the barbed wire fence. But why think of those things? She seldom looked at her back, knew that it was similarly speckled with these small random scars. It wasn't worth the trouble to set up two mirrors to see it.

The "railroad track" was most jarring. It was too perfect, too straight to be mistaken for anything natural. And when she looked at it and ran her fingers along it, she always thought that maybe she could feel the empty spaces inside. She could still hear the surgeon's casual, reassuring tone as he told her what they had needed to remove. "Just a little of your intestines. But don't worry, you have plenty left. We have more than we really need to begin with." And her appendix, which most of her friends had already had removed, anyway. "Redundancy" was the word the surgeon had used.

He didn't tell her at the time about the colostomy. Didn't tell her that she would face several months of the indignity of having to drain her own shit out of a bag. That she would sit in class wondering if the rest of them knew. Oh god, what if they could smell it? Or hear it sloshing around?

She didn't yet realize that it didn't matter. They would all talk about other things. About the cane, or the way she limped. About how she had survived when the others hadn't. But they never talked *to* her. They treated her like she was made of glass and might break if they said the wrong thing. Or fly into a rage. But she wanted to scream at them that all she wanted was for them to just talk to her the way they talked to each other. Complain about how much they hated class or how boring "Ethan Frome" was and how hot Christian Slater was in "Pump Up The Volume." She quickly realized that it was pointless and decided to finish out her senior year in home-schooling. They told her she could graduate with the rest of her class, but she didn't go to the ceremony. She couldn't face the inevitable memorial tributes.

She walked slowly and with deliberation to the bathtub. She had to be careful when she didn't have the leg brace on twisting in the wrong way would cause her knee to give out. She got into the tub and sat down under the shower's spray. She had done this since she was a little girl, even though her father would yell at her about all the water she was wasting. The sound of the shower and the feeling of the water running down over her body calmed and quieted her mind.

She sat, tracing her fingers along her thighs, continuing the tour of her scars. The ones on her thighs were the freshest and the most secret. These she received in her early twenties and not even the doctors had seen them, because these came after the doctor visits, after she was off of her parents' insurance plan. The rows of pale uniform lines running perpendicular along her thighs were methodical. Obsessive. Each one a panic attack. A depressive episode. A dark room and loud music and a razor blade. And the thought that maybe this would be the time that she went too deep and the bleeding wouldn't stop and...

Later, she would have recurring fantasies of cutting her skin off in swatches. Peeling and peeling until she was a raw mass of bloody viscera. It was then that she started writing, channeling these images into surreal hallucinatory stories and poems. Some of her professors were dismayed by her writing, gently suggesting that perhaps she would benefit from the university's counseling program. A few encouraged her, realized that the writing *was* therapeutic for her.

These stories would eventually develop into a vignette in her first book "The Hanging Garden." It tells the story of a beautiful young girl who is in love with a poor peasant boy. Her parents disapprove of their union and arrange for her to be married to a wealthy prince who covets her beauty. The young couple attempt to elope, but are captured by the prince's soldiers. They kill the peasant boy and the girl is forced to marry the prince. On their wedding night, the prince leaves his new princess alone to bathe and tells her to make herself beautiful for him. In despair, she decides to destroy the thing that he loves just as he destroyed the thing she loved. She knows that he loves her only for her physical beauty, so she shatters the mirror in her bathing chamber and using the shards she cuts into her skin. Ripping and peeling her skin off in shreds, until she has flayed herself from the neck down.

Then, she goes to her new husband's chamber where he lays waiting for her. She pads through the room in the dim firelight until she is close enough for him to behold her. She stands before him, wearing her new wedding gown of blood and gore. "Am I beautiful?" she asks as he beholds her. He screams in terror and dies of fright. As the prince's wife, she is next in line to the throne. She orders the finest tailor in the land to make her a beautiful gown of silk and to sew it onto her desecrated body. She wore the gown with a veil to cover her face. The Veiled Queen would become a recurring character in Cassandra's later books. Sometimes a primary character, sometimes peripheral. Sometimes, merely a legend spoken of in whispers.

She sat under the shower for a very long time, trying not to think about anything, until the Xanax made her drowsy enough to go to bed.

# 5

Airports, Cassandra had decided, combined all the things she hated in one place. Crowds, waiting in line, being asked questions, bad music, and bad overpriced food. To say that she was not looking forward to the flight in the morning would be an understatement. But it would take her home, and that was all that she wanted. She had slept well until around 3 AM, when the Xanax started to wear off and she awoke with the cold dull feeling of anxiety in her stomach. Still exhausted, she tried to will herself back to sleep, but gave up after an hour of dozing fitfully for a few minutes at a time and then waking with a start. At around 4:30, she got up and opened her laptop on the table by the window. Looking down at the lights of Manhattan, she tried to write a little. Hoping to make some sense of her thoughts by putting them into words. Nothing came. A few sentence fragments that she would stare at and then delete. There was no sense to be made of her thoughts. Nameless dread and vague worries that didn't even have a source which could be dealt with rationally.

Eventually, she resigned herself to closing the laptop and taking a bath until it was time to get ready. She felt a twinge of guilt that Anthony was sleeping on the couch while she got a bed that she had barely used. Anthony's knock on the door came precisely at 6:00. Military precision as always. The sound of it startled her out of a half-awake insomniac trance, staring at the shimmering light reflecting on her bath water. By the time she had finished bathing, dressed and went out into the living room, Anthony already had a room service tray of croissants and coffee waiting. He had also somehow managed to go back to his own room, shower, shave and put on a new suit in that time.

The croissants were in a basket surrounded by a clean linen napkin, the coffee in a brightly polished carafe. There was also a cut-glass pitcher of orange juice and a plate of fresh strawberries. She couldn't help but think of how much money Sutton House had spent on this room, this entire tour. And she had screwed it all up. They would probably never publish another of her books. They would go through the motions of trying to sell this book, but then politely decline the next one. If she could even bring herself to write another one. Why couldn't they have just left her alone to write?

She slowly chewed small bites of pastry, even though she was not hungry. She sipped her coffee grudgingly, in the way of people who don't want to be awake but have to be. Anthony drank his coffee and didn't eat anything. What and when he ate were largely mysteries to her.

"Did you sleep well?" he asked.

"No." She didn't return the question. Anthony always slept well, no matter what.

"Well, tonight you'll be home and you can sleep in your own bed."

The thought was reassuring, but home seemed so far away. And all she could think of was the ordeal of travel that lay between her and her own safe bed. Anthony was checking his phone, as always. So she knew that he was probably fully abreast of any overnight developments, but was waiting for her to ask before he told her anything.

"So," she asked, after swallowing her coffee. "In the clear light of day, how fucked am I?"

"Not at all, really. George Sutton issued his statement of support. And your books look to have had a nice little spike in Amazon sales this morning."

"Oh, of course they have. Everyone loves a Freakshow. 'Come see the atrocity exhibition!'"

"Now, dear. I know you are more cynical than usual when you are sleep-deprived. But, remember what I told you. People are on your side. They're sympathetic, whether or not you want them to be. And yes, some of the people who are buying your books are curious and are interested in the spectacle. But who cares? Their money spends the same as everyone else's."

After finishing her coffee and giving up on the rest of her croissant, she started to pack up what little of her belongings she had bothered to unpack. When she was little and her family went on trips, her mother would always unpack everything as soon as they checked in, putting her neatly folded clothes in the hotel's dresser drawers. Cassandra always thought this was pointless. Why unpack everything just to pack it all back up in a few days? So, she had always been in the habit of keeping everything in her bags and just digging out whatever she needed. She was slipping her laptop and the book she had brought with her to read, but had made little progress on, into the nice new carry-on bag that she bought specifically for this trip. Anthony called the front desk and requested a cab to take them to the airport. She thought, with slight embarrassment, of the hours she had spent shopping for the carry-on bag online. She didn't have one, because it had been years since she had flown anywhere, and she wanted to buy just the right one. One that would last her for years. And she had only used it for a week and might never use it again. It made her feel foolish to think of herself, imagining that she might start traveling. That this was to be the first of many trips.

She made one last check to make sure she wasn't leaving anything behind, and then they went down in the elevator. In the lobby she lingered near the front door while Anthony returned their keys and signed for the bill. The early morning light from outside already seemed too bright and her head felt foggy from the lack of sleep and she kept going over in her mind all the steps that she would have to go through before she could relax again. Taxi to the airport; flight from New York to Portland, nothing to do there but sit and maybe read a little, maybe try to sleep some; taxi from the airport to Anthony's apartment in Portland. He would ask if she wanted to spend the night there, but she would insist that he drive her home that night; then he would get his car out of the garage and drive her the ninety minutes to her house. She would return the favor and offer to let him stay the night, but he would decline, would want to get back to his own apartment and to his husband, Bart. They would all be back in their own homes where they belonged by midnight, she assured herself. She hoped that they would be able to get her cat out of the boarding kennel that evening. She would have to make sure that Anthony called them and arranged it. She thought of poor Jonas in a cage in a kennel and wished once again that she had never come on this trip.

"Cab's here," Anthony said from behind her. Wordlessly, they walked out toward the taxi as the doorman loaded their bags into the trunk. "Our carriage awaits," she thought. "Our ship. Our steed to carry us home. 'Journeys end in lovers meeting'" she thought, almost deliriously. As she was about to get into the cab, she heard a timid voice behind her.

"Cassandra? Miss Watson, I mean?" She turned and saw Anthony tense up, protective instincts on the alert. The girl was probably in her early twenties, shy, dressed all in black, her hair dyed turquoise blue. She had a copy of "The Coffin-maker's Daughter," Cassandra's second book, clutched tightly in both hands, but Cassandra would have recognized her as one of her readers even without the book. She put her hand on Anthony's arm in a signal to relax.

"Yes?" she asked the young lady.

"I'm sorry to bother you." The young woman could barely make eye contact with Cassandra and her voice trembled, her words spilling out in a nervous rush. "I found out where you were staying. Don't ask how. You're my favorite writer and I had to take a chance to meet you. I was looking forward to the signing for months. I understand why you canceled. I would have too, I can't believe how mean some people can be. I wouldn't be brave enough to do what you do, anyway. But I wanted to meet you so much. I waited out here for hours, hoping I'd see you when you came out. And then when you did, I almost chickened out and didn't say anything."

"I'm not brave," Cassandra said. "I'm running home, scared."

"No. Don't say that. You are so brave to write the way you do. And to go through what you've gone through... you inspire me."

Cassandra didn't know what to say. "Would you like me to sign your book?"

"Yes, please. I'm sorry it's in such bad shape. I've had it since I was twelve. I brought other books, but that one was my first so it's the most important to me."

"What's your name?" asked Cassandra.

"Nicole."

Cassandra wrote on the inside of her book, "To Nicole. You are brave. You are strong. Never forget." And signed her name below.

"You have other books, too?"

Nicole nodded and opened up her shoulder bag. "I have all of them."

Cassandra took each one in turn and signed the inside cover.

"I also have this," said Nicole. "I just got it." She had taken a CD case out of her bag.

"Oh dear God," said Cassandra with an embarrassed laugh. "Where on earth did you get that?"

"eBay."

"What is it?" asked Anthony, looking over Cassandra's shoulder.

"Nothing!" Cassandra tried to shield the CD from him, but he had already seen the cover. It was clearly homemade, printed on an old laser printer, and the black-and-white picture on the cover so faded that it was unrecognizable. The lettering was also faded, but could still be read. It was a colorful scrawl, meant to look like a child's handwriting, and it said "Cassie Eats Cockroaches."

"Is that? No! I've heard of it, but I've never actually seen it!"

"Yes," said Cassandra. "It's my CD. You know, the CD I told you never to ask me about or seek out. Or I would fire you. And possibly stab you thirty or forty times."

"I'm not sayin' a word." Anthony put his hands up in surrender and went over to lean against the cab.

Nicole was looking down at her feet. "I'm sorry, Ms. Watson. I didn't mean to embarrass you. I knew you were in a band in college and I love everything you do, so I had to track it down. Please don't be mad at me."

"Oh, no. I'm not mad at you. Anthony and I just tease each other. And I'm not embarrassed. Well, maybe a little. But, it's not your fault. And please call me Cassandra. Okay?"

"Okay." Nicole was smiling a little now.

"You haven't listened to it, have you?"

"No, not yet. I don't have a CD player."

"Okay. Well, I'll make you a deal. I'll sign it. But, you have to promise me you'll never listen to it. It's absolutely dreadful." Nicole agreed and Cassandra signed. Anthony got to play the bad guy and remind her that they had a plane to catch. Nicole stood on the sidewalk and watched their cab drive away.

They rode for a few minutes in silence, and then Cassandra spoke softly. "That was nice. She was very sweet. Why can't it always be like that?"

"I don't know," said Anthony. "But I am very curious to hear this CD of yours…"

"I know you did a lot of dumb shit in college, too. You're just lucky no one recorded yours."

"So, what does it sound like?"

"It sounds like shit. Kirk, the guitarist, borrowed money from his dad to pay for a couple of hours of studio time when we had only practiced together for like a week. He was obsessed with nine inch nails and Ministry, I was trying to sing like Siouxsie, the bass player only listened to Pantera and we couldn't find a drummer so we used a drum machine that none of us really knew how to program. It was a train wreck. Kirk burned copies of the CD and printed out the inserts on his Mac. He stayed up all night hand-writing his email address on every CD, for all the record execs that he was sure would want to contact him. He gave them to everyone at the couple of shows we played."

"I didn't know you ever played live."

"Yeah, just at a couple of parties. I was so drunk I don't really remember them. It was the only way I could stand to have people look at me. I don't think anyone cared about the music. They were just there to get drunk and see the weird goth girl in her vinyl and fishnets. The whole thing imploded after about six months."

Anthony had his hand over his mouth, trying to stifle a laugh.

"Maybe I should try to find my own copy on eBay," he said.

Cassandra just shook her head.

"Or Youtube. Maybe someone has uploaded it."

She casually gave him the finger as she stared out the window.

# TRACK 3: THE CUTTER

The Huntsman. I see him preparing for his work. A craftsman, readying the tools of his trade. He is bent over a workbench in a shed, a garage, maybe a basement. I see him by candlelight or the flickering light of a lantern. More fittingly it would be the light of a small fire that danced on walls of dripping stone. But, in reality it is more likely a single electric bulb. He works late into the night, lovingly preparing that implement which has become an extension of his body. The limb that he should have been born with and that feels like an amputation when he is not holding it. He sharpens the knife, honing it, caressing it back and forth on the whetstone, and then stropping it on a worn piece of hide until the edge is looking-glass bright.

The knife. It is a Seax. The blade is wide and straight, tapering abruptly to a triangular point. This is the knife that the Vikings carried. And the Saxons, whose name derives from it. True craftsmen, their tool so much a part of their identity that they bear its name. He envies them, aspires to their level of devotion. He sees himself as an inheritor of their legacy, albeit one who is flawed and unworthy. He labors to become one with his tool. He is not satisfied with the tool being an extension of his body. He longs for the day when he becomes the tool that the knife uses to accomplish its tasks. He believes the knife has a will, that it yearns to do the work for which it was forged. A knife longs to cut, as a dancer longs to dance. Was this knife forged from some rare exotic metal by a madman, tempered with brimstone, quenched in the blood of virgins? As much as the writer in me wants that to be true, in reality it was made by an old blacksmith (possibly mad; at the very least quite senile) who lived in the mountains. It was made from a leaf spring from an old Chevy pickup truck. Good high carbon steel. Very resilient, it holds a sharp edge even when cutting through bone and sinew. But it stains easily. The blade wears a mottled patina. The hickory handle is likewise darkened and worn to the shape of its user's hand.

When his tool is ready, when it is sharp enough to shave the hair on his arm, he pulls his hood over his head and sets out to hunt. The night is cold and dark, but the moon is there to guide him. His constant companion, the moon, is to him a blind, faceless, lunatic God. A God that babbles to him a nonsensical chant whose only coherent word is "blood." Yes, the moon craves blood and compels him to hunt and feed its desire. Is he a lycanthrope? Perhaps, in a way, he is. The moon calls to him and makes of him a killer, according to its cycle. Werewolves in legends are almost exclusively male. Were werewolf myths born of men's fear or envy of menstruation? Or were werewolves merely men who still retained a vestigial monthly cycle from that time when they were female in the womb? Who retain an unconscious longing to see blood flow once a month? I digress.

He slips into the darkness, wraps himself in it like a cloak. The darkness is always there, hiding behind the facade of daylight, waiting for him to slip into it like black water. The darkness is patient and eternal. He can feel the darkness around him always and when night falls, and he slips on his cloak of starlight, he feels as though a great tension has been relieved. He sets his foot upon the path.

This is not the forest primeval where the wolf awaited Red Riding Hood. The woods he walks through are thin and scrubby, no more than a half mile across at any point. Choked with cloyingly perfumed honeysuckle and razor wire blackberry brambles. He walks through a shallow, trickling ravine littered with beer cans and condoms. In his mind he sees himself as one of his warrior forebears, traversing the Schwartzwald to do battle, or to fell a hart whose meat will feed his small family. But he knows that he is unworthy of the pristine forest paradise that they called home. He, and the rest of modern humanity, deserve this blighted, obscene parody of a forest. It is their punishment for their degeneracy. Humans were given a Paradise in which to live and chose to make a Perdition of it. The others delude themselves, living in a fool's paradise. But he knows the truth. This is Hell. And if he must live in Hell, he will embrace the darkness and the blood and the fire. He will live as a Devil.

He leaves the ravine and comes out into his hunting ground: the gravel lot beside the cemetery. Even though it's a weeknight, he knows that there will be prey here. A small car, some cheap model from the mid-70s, sits at the far edge of the lot, away from the lone security light. When the wind shifts he smells the sweet skunky smell of marijuana smoke. Teenagers engaged in debauchery, just as he knew they would be. He creeps closer to the car, enjoying the rush of adrenaline, his heart pounding in his ears. Heel-toe to keep his footfalls from crunching on the gravel. Quiet, like his father taught him on boyhood hunting trips. He hefts the knife easily in his hand, waiting for it to tell him what it wants of him. He comes close enough to the car to touch its cold metal flank. He can make out the dark outline of two people in the front of the car. Is he disappointed that he can't see any nude flesh? Does the sight of nubile teenage skin titillate him, add to the thrill? Or is his repulsion for his fellow man so complete that it has overwhelmed even his most primal urges? I don't know, my writerly empathy only goes so far. I can't bring myself to look that deeply into his mind.

The two teenagers in the car are Mary Jenkins and Tommy McDowell, both seventeen. They are sharing a joint and some warm beer and she is giving him a reluctant blowjob. This is as far as I can go, though. What happened to them, I can't bring myself to fictionalize. Because this is where it becomes real. This is where it turns into the tragic story of two kids who didn't deserve to die. Tommy went to a different school, so I didn't know him. And Mary was only a passing acquaintance, someone I saw in the halls at school, but never really talked to. But we occupied the same spaces, used the same bathroom stalls, and sat in the same chairs in the cafeteria. I probably ate off the same tray that she did at some point. Maybe I'm a coward and maybe I'm a bad writer, but I can't bring myself to speculate on what the last, horrific minutes of their lives were like. Good writers don't flinch, someone once said. Fair enough, but I'm flinching. I'm no Jack Ketchum.

All I can do is relate the facts that I know. Tommy had his throat slit, probably through the open driver's side window. He was found sitting upright, with his dick out and blood covering the front of his torso. His death was quick, a formality. Like a skillful butcher dispatching a hog so swiftly that it is dead before it feels the blade on its neck. The Huntsman's male victims always went quick. But he took his time with the females. Mary was found fifty yards away from the car. She made a run for it. But it must have been in blind panic. She was found at the base of a mausoleum and head trauma indicated that she ran into the stone wall in the dark and knocked herself out cold. Hopefully out cold anyway. I hope that she had a few minutes of unconscious respite from the fear and the pain. The part I try to keep myself from wondering about is if she had her head in Tommy's lap when his throat was cut. Was she performing that act which would have someday become tender and loving had she lived long enough to learn that sex was supposed to be mutual and not coerced or cajoled? Did she hear him squeal and feel his hot blood rain down on the back of her head? I shouldn't wonder about this; she deserves better than this lurid speculation. She deserved better than to die in terror on cold graveyard dirt. But that is where she was found. And like all the other girls, he took his time. He made her hurt for a while before it was over. If she was unconscious at some point, she was awake by the end. Then he hacked her chest open and cut out her heart, like all the others.

He skulks back through the darkness to his lair, his newest trophy warm in his hand. He puts it on display with all the rest. Where did he keep them? In jars lining a shelf? I should like that, I think. Little glass caskets for all of his stolen hearts.

Am I romanticizing this man, this killer? How can I not? He is the most important person in my life. I know next to nothing about him, but he had a more profound influence on me than my mother or my father or any friend or lover in my life. He made me the person I am today. He molded me, shaped me, carved me. I see the marks of his handiwork on my flesh every time I disrobe. He lives in a dark recess of my brain and always will and sometimes he whispers to me. What choice do I have but to speculate about him, fantasize about him and obsess over him like the object of a schoolgirl crush? I hate him. I hate him like the devout hate the Devil. And like them, my Devil influences every action and every decision I make. But in a way I am more fortunate than them. They believe that The Devil is real, but they don't know for sure. I know. I got to meet my Devil.

# 6

Cassandra owned a house in a small town on the Oregon coast, ninety miles from Portland. She had bought it outright in 2005, flush with money from the sale of movie rights to one of her books. The movie never got made, but the house was hers. Foulweather Bay was a small town with little to attract tourists. Most of her neighbors were either retirees or wealthy families from the city who only used their beach houses for a few weekends a year. Further inland, where the forest started, and the ground began to slope up towards the mountains, were a few scattered mobile homes belonging to loggers and commercial fishermen. Some of her neighbors knew that Cassandra was a writer of some kind, but if any of them had read her books, they made no mention of it. They gave her privacy, which was what she had been looking for when she moved there. A little house by the sea, where she could be alone and write. Walk on the beach if she chose or just sit by the window and watch the winter storms batter the coastline.

The house itself was little more than a cottage. Cassandra had painted it in shades of gray and black and dark blue. A few accents of purple. It was like living in a rain cloud, she sometimes thought. My little fairytale cottage by the sea. "By the sounding sea," she amended. The walls were adorned with art, cheap posters mixed indiscriminately with original prints that were, in some cases, quite valuable. She had framed original paintings of some of her older book covers (the newer ones all used digital art). And everywhere: books. On shelves, in piles. Single books left in random places.

Scattered around on various shelves and cases and sideboards were animal skulls, from massive antlered elk down to a delicate eggshell-thin bird skull in a glass cloche. Colored glass bottles. Candle-holders of brass and iron. Incense burners. A bouquet of dried roses in a thrift store vase. And Halloween decorations, vintage, modern, cheap, collectible. All the accumulated ephemera of a lifetime scattered around to make the house look as much like the inside of her head as possible.

"I am home. This is my place. This is where I belong. I am strong here. I am safe here." She had repeated this mantra to herself countless times since returning from the ill-fated book tour. She could feel her strength coming back, just being at home. Sitting on her small back patio, listening to the waves. Or watching Jonas as he intently studied the fascinating array of birds outside his window. The rest of the world felt farther and farther away. "We're all alone, here on the moon, Jonas," she said as she stroked his back. Jonas paid no attention though, as he was occupied with watching a hummingbird that was undoubtedly up to no good.

Anthony made the drive from Portland to Foulweather Bay once a week to check on her and keep her updated on how her career was going. But, mostly he managed her affairs from his apartment and communicated with her by e-mail. They had once had a routine they would perform upon his arrival that consisted of Cassandra demanding that he tell her all about the exciting goings-on in the big city; about the latest scandals and all the elegant balls and the new plays at the "thea-tuh" this season. She would in turn tell him of all the small town gossip; exaggerated soap opera versions of small town life, mixed with her own mordant creativity. "Oh, the whole town is positively in an uproar, because the Jenkins boy got the Cummins girl pregnant. And then wouldn't you know it, he went and got eaten by a Sea Monster before he could marry her!" After a few years, the routine grew tiresome. Now, when he came to visit, it was all business.

She had told Anthony when he dropped her off that she wouldn't need him for at least a week. Assured him over and over that she would be fine and that he should just stay home and spend time with Bart. She did ask that he call Mrs. Ledesma and see if she could come by in a few days. Martha Ledesma was a housekeeper for several of the local families. She came to Cassandra's house once a week to do a little cleaning and then go to the grocery store for her. Martha sometimes offered to cook dinner for Cassandra, but Cassandra usually declined. Sometimes, though, Martha would bring by a huge batch of homemade tamales, which Cassandra accepted eagerly and would happily live on for days. Martha's husband, Jose, was a commercial fisherman who would go to sea for a month at a time, and Cassandra soon learned that Martha's gifts of food coincided with the periods when he was gone. She clearly missed having someone to cook for.

A couple of times a year Cassandra would also pay Jose to do some work at her house; cleaning the gutters, pressure-washing the walkways, repairing any roof leaks or missing shingles that had developed throughout the year. She liked the Ledesmas because they were cheerful people and they didn't ask her questions. Martha had thankfully gotten over her habit of crossing herself every time she entered the house. Although, sometimes Cassandra still got the distinct feeling that Martha regarded her as one of those spoiled rich Gringos who worries way too much about everything.

The cottage had a small but well-appointed kitchen. And Cassandra enjoyed cooking. Although, when she was intent on her work, she would sometimes subsist on frozen dinners and canned soup for days at a time. Since returning from New York, she had found little motivation for either cooking or writing. Trying to get back to her routine, she would sit at her desk every evening with a document open and stare at the screen, trying to arrange her thoughts into some sort of pattern that she could write out into a story. She had never suffered from writer's block before; quite the contrary, her fear had always been that she wouldn't be able to write all the stories crowding around in her head. She realized now that writer's block wasn't a lack of ideas, but rather a stubborn refusal of those ideas to arrange themselves coherently. After an hour or so of fruitlessly wrestling with her thoughts, she would inevitably give up and tell herself that no one cared, anyway. People didn't care about her stories anymore, they only cared about the lurid details of her past. Even when she tried to picture in her mind Nicole, there on the street in Manhattan, nervously professing her admiration, all she could think was that anything she wrote now would only be a disappointment. "Better that you grow up now, little Nicole, and learn that there are much better writers out there. I should have given her something by Flannery O'Connor and told her 'read this and never look back.'"

"I am a shell now," she thought. "I am a revenant. A ghost. The real me died in New York. Or is lost there still, trying to find her way back, and this changeling was returned in her place. I'll never write again. I'll comb the beaches every day and collect driftwood and shells to sell to the tourists who take pity on a crazy old woman. Or I'll simply wait for starvation to come and then Jonas can eat my remains." Even this, she knew, was a rambling mish-mash of melodramatic symbolism unworthy of her literary reputation. She tried to re-read some of the formative books that had inspired her as a young writer, hoping they would re-ignite that spark. "The Bloody Chamber" and "Outer Dark" and "Geek Love." Anne Sexton and Charles Perrault and Andrew Lang and the original uncensored Brothers Grimm. "Snow White, Blood Red" and "Snow, Glass, Apples." But these only served to discourage her more and to make her think of her own work as a pale imitation of the masters.

The night before Anthony's next scheduled visit, she sat for a long time thinking about how she would tell him that it was over. She had become certain that she would never be able to write again. She would live on whatever dwindling royalties still came in from her previous books. Anthony was technically her agent, so he was entitled to fifteen percent of all of her earnings. But she also paid him a salary on top of that to act as some combination of manager, personal assistant, and often her only link to the rest of humanity. But, inevitably, she would no longer be able to pay him for these services and he would have to take on other clients. That had been the arrangement that Cassandra insisted on. She would pay him a comfortable salary in exchange for his dedication to her as his only client. When the money finally stopped coming in, she would… well, she wasn't sure what she would do. Sell the house and move to a small apartment and become a crazy cat lady, maybe.

She slept fitfully and awoke around noon. Anthony would arrive precisely at 1:00. He always arrived precisely on time, regardless of weather or traffic conditions. Cassandra had become convinced that he left hours earlier than necessary in case there was traffic and then parked somewhere and waited so he wouldn't be early. While she awaited his arrival, she walked outside to retrieve the mail from the box by the road.

Anthony would deliver the bulk of her mail, which came to her official address, a post office box in Portland. Very few people knew her home address, so the box generally only contained advertisements.

But today, among the coupons for the grocery store and the pizza restaurant in the larger town twenty miles away, was a letter. Her name and address were hand-written and there was no return address. It was postmarked Dark Hollow Falls, Virginia. The town she had grown up in and hadn't been back to in over a decade. Some cousin or aunt that had somehow gotten her address? "Hey, I saw you on the TV. You should come to the family reunion next year." Or someone's wedding. Or it would be just a blatant plea for money. She ripped it open and found a single sheet of paper with one sentence written on it.

When Anthony arrived, she was at the kitchen table staring at the piece of paper. She barely acknowledged his arrival, and when he asked her what she was looking at, she showed him the envelope. "This," she said. "It came in the mail."

"Okay. So what does it say?" She handed him the sheet of paper and he read it. "'I'll fall with your knife.' What the hell does that mean?"

"It's the name of a song. Peter Murphy. It's one of my favorites."

"Peter Murphy? He was... wait, don't tell me.. Sisters of Mercy?"

Cassandra rolled her eyes and gave an exaggerated sigh. "Bauhaus! Andrew Eldritch was in the Sisters!"

"Right, Bauhaus. I knew that."

She shook her head. "How can someone who doesn't know the difference between Bauhaus and The Sisters of Mercy work for me?"

"Hey, back then I was listening to Public Enemy and N.W.A."

"Sure you were. Boyz II Men is more like it."

"Sure Boyz II Men was good for when I wanted to get with the ladies. Back before I figured out that ladies weren't what I was interested in."

Cassandra smiled. It had been a long time since they had joked and teased each other about what an odd couple they made. It lifted her spirits and made her think that despite having no romantic interest in each other, they really were like an old married couple.

"But, anyway," she went on. "That was one of my favorite songs in college. I used to listen to it constantly. It made me cry. But, I haven't listened to it in years. So, how the hell would someone know about it? And get my home address?"

"Crazy fan, I guess. People can learn a lot about you on the Internet. Did you ever mention the song in an interview?"

"No. I don't think so."

"Could just be a lucky guess. You've made references to Murphy's songs in your work, right? And unfortunately, these days, if someone wants to find out your home address there's not much that can be done about it."

"It's postmarked Dark Hollow Falls! I promise you, no one in that town reads my books. Nicholas Sparks is more their speed."

"Probably just someone who's obsessed with you and your... past, who made some kind of pilgrimage to where it all started."

"'Just someone who's obsessed' he says. Oh, is that all? Just someone who is obsessed with the horrible murder of my best friends? No big deal."

"Well, yeah. It's not really that bad, relatively speaking. There are people out there who idolize the Columbine killers. There are people who look at serial killers like rock stars. This is probably just someone who likes your books and has a weird misguided way of expressing their admiration. I'll contact law enforcement, just to be safe, but I really don't think it's anything to worry about. Give me the letter. I'll turn it over to the police. Wait, does this town even have a police department?"

"I don't think so."

"Okay, then I'll talk to the sheriff's department. Or maybe the state police. And maybe if you get another letter like that, you should call them before you open it."

She put her head in her hands and rubbed her temples. "It's never going to end, is it? It'll just go on and on and it will never let me rest."

"Now, let's not start that again. You're still not completely recovered from the stress of the book tour. You just need some more time to get back to normal."

"I can't write, Anthony! I've never had writer's block before, but I can't get a single word on the page. Nothing will come, because I can't think of anything except... you know."

She went to the window where Jonas sat monitoring the activities of the chipmunks in the front yard. "I can't get away from him. I thought he was dead and gone, but I didn't do a good enough job. I should have... cut his head off. Cut his heart out and buried it in salt with a stake of holly in it. Stuffed his corpse with garlic and wolfsbane. I should have known he'd come back."

"Him? You're talking about..."

"Yes. Him. The Huntsman. I haven't even spoken his name in over a decade, for fear that I would invoke him and give him power again."

"You're being ridiculous. He's long dead. He's not some super human killer who keeps coming back from the grave. This isn't a slasher movie."

"I know he hasn't come back to life physically. But spiritually he never really died. His spirit went into me and I've never exorcised it. I just tried to ignore it and hoped it would go away. But he put a part of himself into me, even as he was dying. That's what real monsters do, Anthony. The monsters in storybooks kill you or eat you or keep you as a pet. But what the real monsters do is much worse. They make you one of them."

# TRACK 4: SPELLBOUND

(Fragments from Cassandra's journal.)

The midwife bustles through the door of The Sorceress's little hovel in the woods. She shakes off the storm and holds the bundle to her chest and then reluctantly hands it over. The Sorceress unwraps the limp white form. A stillborn child, still warm from its mother's womb. The midwife is shooed away clutching in her hand the gold piece, a year's wages, almost. The midwife would have to leave, move to some other town. She would never be able to show her face there again after her betrayal.

The Sorceress lays the little body on the rough oaken planks of her table. A candle stub gutters on the mantle, sending up tendrils of oily black smoke. The knife, a shard of obsidian, catches the meager light. The edge is as sharp as broken glass. She draws it across the delicate little belly and it cleaves open as easily as risen bread dough. Plunges her hand in and draws out the entrails into a clay bowl. Much can be foretold from reading the entrails of animals. But those of humans are better. And these, that have never breathed air, never digested even mother's milk, are the best of all.

She kneads her hands into the warm slimy mass. Feeling the lobes and twists. Reading in them omens and portents. Her breath catches. She feels something hard in one of the intestines. Pushes it out through the delicate lining. A small stone, no bigger than a pea. Bezoars are common to find in the entrails of goats and oxen and they have great power. They can cure poisons. To find one in the innards of an unborn child is unheard of. This object will serve her very well. She holds it in her palm like a rare gem. The gold piece that she had charmed away from a traveling merchant was well spent.

The rest of the little body will not go to waste. She will render its fat to make a candle that, if burned under a full moon, will give her the gift of flight. Eat its eyes to gain second sight. Tan its delicate skin to make a purse that will double any object put inside it. And the tiny eggshell skull will sit beatifically on her shelf like an idol.

The Sorceress haunts the night forests. Weary travelers have sometimes spied her hooded form along the dark roadsides and rumors abound that she can see in the dark. But she has no need of sight. She navigates by scent and by sound. She knows these woods so well that the trees make their presence known to her. They are her family and friends, which no human has ever been to her. They alert her to any alien presence amongst them. They whisper to her of an intruder.

He stands silently amongst the swaying pines. He wears a leather cloak with the hood pulled down over his eyes. His face is obscured by a shadow that even the Sorceress's heightened senses cannot penetrate.

"Who are you that haunts my woods?"

When he speaks, his breath is sepulchral and his voice is like the sound of every lecherous insinuation, every sadistic taunt ever spoken by man, combined into one. "I am The Huntsman."

"What business do you have here?"

"I hunt."

"You poach. The animals in this wood are my charges. You do not have my permission to harm them."

The wind shifts and she smells him. He smells of blood upon blood. New blood and old. He smells of soil and sweat and iron and smoke. She smells fresh blood and sees - senses- a small shape at his feet. A doe, freshly killed. Her fury grows slowly, like a spark being whipped into flame by the wind.

"You have taken what is not yours. You have taken from me without permission. A price must be paid. What do you offer in exchange?"

He stands motionless. "I have nothing to offer except death."

"Very well. I accept your offer. Bring me the heart of a young maiden."

He nods and stalks off into the night. She crouches above the doe and speaks an incantation in a voice that no human ear can hear. She is ensuring that the doe's spirit has everything it needs to continue its journey. She gently closes its eyes with her fingers. As she walks away, wolves descend on the little body and feast.

Later that night The Huntsman comes to her home and stands holding a small glass box. He hands it to her and inside is a bright red heart still beating. She places it on her shelf next to the skillets and silks and carvings. He stands waiting and the stench of death clings to him like a miasma of disease.

"Now," she says. "You will bring me another. And another, until I feel that your debt is repaid. But you will never hunt another animal. You will only hunt humans, because they are as cowardly as you. You don't deserve to hunt the noble beasts of the forest. You are beneath them."

He nods and steps back into the eternal night....

The Huntsman exists in a land of eternal darkness. Cold and mist. Blood and fire and death. He wanders lost and alone through a forest, with the blade as his only companion. Skulls grow amongst the gnarled tree trunks. Streams of blood run down the rocks. He neither sleeps nor ever rests, walking endlessly. This is his perdition, for failing to kill C____ and deliver her heart to the Sorceress. In and amongst the trees he sees faces. They scream at him soundlessly. They wear expressions of pain and anguish. The spectres of countless victims, the ragged gaping maws at their throats and in their chests, that bleed eternally.

They never leave him, but he is alone. Alone with his hate and the violence that it has wrought. After an eon of walking, he calls to the Sorceress and pleads with her to let him rest at last. She comes to him and looks down on him in bemusement.

"Is this not what you wanted?" she asks. "You wanted a world of blood and I gave it to you. You hungered for death and I have prepared for you an endless feast of it. Do you grow weary of the pain? Are you ungrateful of my gifts?"

"No," she says. "You are not ready."

The Sorceress vanishes and The Huntsman walks on....

# 7

The extra room in the cottage, the one that the real estate agent had so enthusiastically told Cassandra would make a great nursery, was used for storage. Stacks of cardboard boxes, filled with old business papers, copies of her books in various languages, writing awards she had won through the years, old mementos. She dug through these until she found the boxes she was looking for. The oldest boxes, the ones that had gone through a half dozen moves, been shoved under beds and into closets and been mended with duct tape where their corners had split. She hadn't opened these boxes in years, but she knew what they contained. Knew that when she opened them, they would release the smells of her old bedroom and her dorm room. And her first apartment, a dump that was little more than a single room in an old house full of crazy people who thought they were artists and where she lived for years until Anthony had exasperatedly told her that she had way too much money to be living in a place like that. She hadn't even realized she wasn't poor anymore.

The very oldest box didn't concern her. She had gotten it when she was twelve, a copy paper box from the paper mill where her grandfather worked. It contained all of her "little girl" things, the things that she had decided that she was too old for. Toy ponies and dolls that smelled like strawberries. Charm bracelets and makeup sets and tiny glass bottles of perfume that would turn her stomach if she smelled them now. Pretty smooth rocks and feathers and pieces of colorful glass, treasures found on adventures in the woods. She had gone through this box a few times over the years, rescuing those items that had taken on new meaning and displaying them like amulets on the shelves of her writing room.

The box that interested her now was newer. A vodka box from some liquor store. She took it and put it on her desk and then went back for the crate that had been underneath it. A milk crate from a dairy that had gone out of business in the 80s. It was where she had kept her records since she was a teenager. They had collected dust since she switched to CDs and eventually to streaming. She took this into the office as well, being reminded of how heavy and bulky records were, and why she had stopped buying them in the first place. She sat at the desk and began in a ritualistic fashion to remove the items in the box. She took the time to hold each, to feel its power and remember its significance. The high school year-book, which she had never opened. The envelope full of photos that she set aside to look at later. The old incense burners and tarot cards. The worn copy of "Buckland's Complete Book of Witchcraft." The boxcutter with inter-changeable blades. A Zippo lighter and an old hash pipe. A leather choker with an ankh pendant. An old leather-bound sketchbook that she had used as a journal, containing some of her earliest attempts at writing.

A folder with a few concert fliers. One was for one of the few shows her band ever played. It was in someone's base-ment, opening for a nationally touring industrial band, whose lead singer tried to get her to have sex with him by telling her that he knew Trent Reznor. She found out years later that the singer had become a Science Fiction writer and a notorious White Supremacist.

No newspaper clippings. If this were a movie, she thought, this box would be full of newspapers whose headlines would conveniently tell the viewers everything they need to know about my backstory. Convenient exposition is so rare in real life. This last flier, though. Zoom in, linger on it. It is worn and faded. Xeroxed on cheap paper. Thumbtack holes at the corners. Creases where it was folded up and stuck in a pocket years ago. The flier is for the band Danzig, playing at a club called The Flood Zone in Richmond, Virginia. The date: November 6th 1990. *The* date, of course. The night when everything happened, everything changed. The last night of my life, she thinks.

All that was left was the envelope of pictures. But she didn't want to look at those yet. It wasn't right yet. She wanted to wait until Anthony returned from the errand she had sent him on. "I need you to do something for me," she had said. "I need you to go get me a record player."

"A record player? I'd have to go back to Portland. There's nowhere here on the coast that would sell them. Maybe an antique shop, but those would all be closed by now. I can come back tomorrow, I guess. Or we can order one online and have it delivered day after tomorrow."

"No, I need one tonight."

"Why do you need one tonight?" he asked, trying not to sound like a long-suffering parent.

"There's something I have to listen to. It's important, trust me."

"I guarantee you that any song you want to listen to is available on YouTube."

"Just do this for me, okay?"

"Okay, I'll try." He knew the stubborn tone in her voice and had learned that there was no point in trying to reason with her when she had her mind set on something.

He had been gone for over two hours and she didn't expect him back any time soon. She began to flip through the records that she had kept all these years, even after her last turntable stopped working and she gave it away rather than trying to fix it. Running her fingers over the covers and reading the titles: Tinderbox. First and Last and Always. Mask. Pornography. Phantasmagoria. Tender Prey. She didn't notice the sound of Anthony's car pulling into the driveway, and was slightly startled to hear the front door open.

"I didn't expect you back so soon."

"I didn't expect me back so soon either." He was carrying an old Technics turntable that looked like it was from the 80s, if not older. "I had all but resigned myself to driving back to Portland, finding a record shop that was still open and then driving back here and not getting home until after midnight. But then inspiration struck! I found an old guy in Newport who had a record player for sale on Craigslist. I had to offer him more than he was asking, because he really didn't want me to come to his house until tomorrow. He said that six in the evening was 'too late to do business.' I think the real problem was that he was already completely baked. I gave him some story about needing it for a party tonight. And paid him an extra fifty dollars for his trouble. He lives in an old house way out in the woods. And once I got there, he talked my ear off about vintage stereo equipment and didn't want to let me leave. I should have been back here an hour ago."

Cassandra went to the kitchen and heated up a can of soup and made grilled cheese sandwiches, while Anthony figured out how to get the record player to connect to her home theater system. "Well, you're in luck," he called through the doorway. "Since you have an older receiver, it has an input for the record player. Otherwise we would have to get a preamp. And there's no way I could have gotten one of those tonight."

She set sandwiches and bowls of soup on the table for the two of them. Anthony tossed his tie over his shoulder so he wouldn't drip soup on it. He still dipped his sandwich in the soup, though. Cassandra ate quickly. She hadn't eaten anything all day, but it hadn't occurred to her how hungry she was until she smelled the food cooking.

It had started to rain softly and the breeze through the open window carried in the gentle sound of wind chimes. Jonas slept in a ball in his little bed by the unlit fireplace. They didn't speak until after they had finished eating, and Cassandra carried their plates to the kitchen.

"Okay," she said. "Remind me how to use this thing."

Anthony showed her how to switch the receiver to "Phono" mode and how to switch on the record player. "Not much to it. Do you remember how to find the start of a song, look for the groove?"

"I think so. It should be like riding a bike, right?" She was digging out the record that she had been looking for. The cover was an abstract design of blues and purples, with the word "Cascade" written across the bottom. She set it on the turntable and, after a few miscues, found the start of the song she was looking for. "This is the song my mystery letter-writer wanted me to listen to. So we're gonna listen to it."

Anthony was surprised. What he knew of Cassandra's taste in music was generally dark and intense. But this was a light, hopeful, upbeat pop song. It was pretty. When it was done playing and Cassandra lifted the needle, he said as much. "I was expecting something much darker."

"I love that song. It was my light, during a very dark time in my life. I spent most of college and grad school wallowing in that darkness. Numbing myself with alcohol and drugs. Pretending to be a slut, because the attention made me feel beautiful. But never putting out, because I couldn't stand the idea of anyone touching me or even seeing me naked. And then this album came out. It was given to me by Kirk, the guitarist from my band. He got it for me while he was in Europe on vacation with his family and gave it to me when we came back from Summer break. I listened to 'I'll Fall With Your Knife' more times than I can count and I cried every time. Because it is so beautiful. And because Peter Murphy was like an old friend and I felt like that song was him trying to tell me to be happy. It didn't work, but it pulled me from the darkness a little.

"And slowly I learned to push the darkness away. To capture it in my stories and hold it there. You know I used to practice witchcraft. Eventually, writing became a form of witchcraft for me. Each book was a spell, a ritual. A way to protect myself from the darkness. I created these little worlds and filled them with the blood and the blackness and then I slammed the door shut on them. They created a web of protection around me and around this house. But I realize now that I broke the spell by going back out into the world. The door is open, and the darkness has flooded back in.

"I was planning on telling you that I was retiring from writing. That I couldn't bring myself to write another word and that I wouldn't be able to pay you anymore. That was my plan until I got that letter. And then it all became clear. The spell has been broken, and I have called him back to life."

"The Huntsman?"

"Yes."

"What the Hell are you talking about? He's dead. You can't bring someone back from the dead."

Cassandra shook her head. "Not literally, maybe. But I allowed his... spirit. Essence, I don't know what, to come back into the world. And I know what I have to do. So, now I'm telling you that you win. You get what you want."

"And what is that?"

"I'm going to write about it. I'm going to write the thing you've been trying to get me to write for fifteen years. I don't know if it will be anything that any publisher will want. I don't know if it will be what you were hoping for. But I know that it's the only thing I can write about now. I have to cast the spell again to hold the darkness back."

"Well," said Anthony cautiously. "If you think it will help. I think it will be healthy for you to write about it. But, you know I don't want you to do anything that will upset you. I know you haven't thought about these things in a long time."

Cassandra laughed. "These things are all I think about. I have even written about it before. Or tried to. Just sketches. Very abstract ones at that. I never told you about them. And I could never bring myself to write about it too explicitly, for fear that to evoke his name was to give him power. But now I know it's too late. He has power once again. Or always did. So I will write about him. I will cast my spell against him. It may very well be the last thing I ever write. But, I have to write it and I have to start tonight."

# TRACK 5: ALL WE EVER WANTED WAS EVERYTHING

Elise was always the first to try new things. She was a year older, for one thing. We met in first grade and she had already been held back a year at that point. Too many absences and delayed verbal development. She was fearless and rambunctious and practically feral. She lived alone with her mom. Jenny was the "cool mom" who had gotten pregnant at sixteen and still liked rock music and partying and let you get away with things. Stay up too late and have a sip of beer, watch scary movies and promise not to tell.

The other moms didn't like her, partially because she was a bad influence and partially because of the way their husbands looked at her. I loved her and thought she was the coolest person on earth. A queen, and Elise her princess. Nights that my mom would allow me to spend at her house were the most exciting of my childhood. We would eat pizza and watch horror movies and listen to her mom's music and then camp out in our sleeping bags on the back deck. Counting stars and falling asleep in the smell of honeysuckle and the sound of whippoorwills. It was heaven for two little girls in rural Virginia in 1985.

Elise and I were yin and yang, two sides of the same whole.

Light and dark, but in truth we were both a combination of light and dark in different measure. She tanned easily and her natural blond hair got lighter in the summer sun. I was brown-haired and fair skinned and burned if I didn't wear sunscreen. I was quiet and loved horses and cats and books. Unicorn stickers on my notebooks and posters for "Labyrinth" and "The Dark Crystal" on my bedroom wall. She acted out and craved attention and lived to push boundaries and get in trouble. But there was a quiet, sad part of her that only I ever saw. And inside me there was an anger and a darkness that only she ever saw. We knew all of each other's secrets. But I'll never tell. I'll take hers to the grave, because she took mine to the grave.

Elise was the first to discover glam metal. Her mom was one of the first people in our town to get a satellite dish, and the first to get MTV. Elise was obsessed. It was fast and loud and dangerous and she was in love. Until then, we both listened to whatever was on the radio. Michael Jackson, Madonna, Prince. But then Elise introduced me to Poison and Warrant and Cinderella. They looked like nothing we had seen before, pretty boys in makeup singing about sex. My mom hated it, but Elise's mom was right there on the couch beside her. She bought Poison and Warrant's tapes and would blast them from the stereo of her little Honda when she came to pick us up from school. She taught us how to tease our hair and do our makeup. Soon Elise discovered Guns n Roses, and she loved them even more. Because they were more dangerous, more overtly sexual. Elise was never satisfied, always looking for something that went farther.

Then, in 1989, I discovered my own love. My family still didn't have MTV, so Elise would record it for me. She'd take some old VHS tape that had previously contained footage of a family picnic or a dubbed copy of a movie that no one liked anymore and record hours of music videos for me. She tried to curate them at first, but eventually she started just popping the tape in the VCR and letting it record until it came to the end. I would fast forward through the commercials and the talking and the videos I knew I didn't like. If something I liked came up, I would watch it and then rewind it back and watch it again. Over and over and over.

Sometimes, something I didn't recognize would come on and I would stop and watch if it looked interesting. I still remember fast forwarding and suddenly seeing images of shadows and lace and spider webs. Pale men with black hair and dark circles under their eyes. I was intrigued, so I stopped, rewound and watched it from the beginning. It was by a band I had heard of, whose shirts I had seen people wear. But, I had never heard their music. The song was dark, but it wasn't aggressive. It shambled along at a mournful pace. It was nothing like the songs I had loved before, but it was like finding something that I didn't know I had been looking for. That video changed my life. It was "Lullaby" by The Cure and it gave me nightmares for a week. But I was in love.

I was fascinated. It was like a creepy bedtime story set to music and Robert Smith was like a dark Fairy Tale version of the metal pretty boys we loved. I know it wasn't this immediate, but when I think back I see it as a switch being thrown, after which everything changed. It all came together. The dark fantasy movies and stories I loved. My infatuation with Lydia from "Beetlejuice" and Lili from the movie "Legend." What my parents, with nervous laughter, referred to as my "morbid streak."

There was a cemetery between my house and Elise's and for years it had been our meeting place. Initially, because it was a convenient place halfway between our houses. A pathway through the woods ran behind the cemetery. We would meet at the back fence and sometimes we would walk in the woods and play in the creek and pick blackberries from the briars and eat them until our mouths were stained purple and our arms were spider-webbed with scratches. And sometimes we would walk and play or sit and talk amongst the headstones. Elise liked it because it was private. Grown ups didn't look for us there and we seldom saw anyone else. We could hide behind the oldest mausoleums at the back of the cemetery and talk about anything without fear of being overheard. Later, it became our spot to smoke cigarettes that Elise stole from her mother's purse. And later still we would have "kissing practice" so we would know what to do when we had boyfriends.

I honestly don't think Elise ever put much thought into what was buried beneath our feet, or sealed up in those stone buildings. We may as well have been in a park. But, for me, there was more to it. I felt a power and an energy there. Death always fascinated me. It scared me, sure, but I had always been drawn to the things that scared me. My mother always said I had to touch the stove, because I didn't believe people when they told me it was hot. When I had a toothache, I couldn't keep myself from probing it with my tongue, just to feel that sharp jolt of pain. When I got a cut, I would be mesmerized by the scarlet trickle running on my skin. And when I began to menstruate, that scarlet flow fascinated me and repulsed me in equal measure.

Ghost stories and "Scary Stories To Tell In The Dark" gave me nightmares, but I always wanted more. Looking back, I think I always wished to be the monster, because it's better to be the one doing the scaring than the one who is scared. Being in the cemetery scared me a little, but it was also exciting and energizing. I used to say that I was born Goth. When I discovered the music and the fashion, when I started dyeing and teasing my hair and put on the makeup, I was taking off a costume and finally showing the world my true face.

It was okay that Elise wasn't into it in the same way I was.

It was the first thing that I loved on my own. It made it seem special and private. At the same time, it was wonderful to learn that there were other people out there like me who loved the same things I did. It was the first thing that ever made me feel like I made sense. I wanted more.

The next week after I saw that video, I convinced Elise to make a pilgrimage with me to a store called Dark Planet Records, in the next town over. The "big town," Annesville, which had all of forty thousand people, not counting college students. Dark Planet was a small independent store that mostly catered to the students. We had only been there a few times before to look around. We felt out of place and the students regarded most "townies" as rednecks and looked down their noses at us. We had looked through their metal selection a few times, but most of it was bands we had never heard of. The store always smelled like incense and cigarettes, and they always seemed to be playing R.E.M. over the stereo system. We hated R.E.M. We would always end up leaving and going to the chain record store in the mall, where we felt more welcome. But, once I discovered The Cure, I knew Dark Planet would have more of what I was looking for. When we were younger, we would have Elise's mom drive us to Annesville to hang out. But that Summer I had turned 15 and got my learner's permit. My older brother had joined The Navy and given me his car. Elise was older and already had her license, so I could drive as long as she was in the car with me.

While Elise looked at the posters in the back of the store, looking bored and pretending not to notice the college guys checking her out, I made my way straight to the shelf marked "C." Flipping through the records towards the back, almost to "D," Culture Club, The Cult, and there: The Cure. They had several albums, and I had to read the track listings of all of them to find "Lullaby." I didn't know what any of their other songs sounded like, so I had to get the record that at least had one song I knew. I read the title: "Disintegration." The cover art was everything I could have hoped for, Robert Smith's face, spectral pale and surrounded by hallucinatory flowers.

I was debating whether I should buy one of their other albums as well. What if I don't like the rest of the music? What if I love it and want more and then I have to wait another week to get the other albums? I was jolted out of my indecision by a voice behind me.

"Excuse me." I turned around and when I saw her, I think I may have gasped. God, I hope I didn't, but that's how I remember it. She was absolutely beautiful. Jet black hair and ivory skin. Cat's eye makeup and black lipstick. Black nail polish. Black, lacy, flowing dress over combat boots. She was everything I wanted to be. Even before I had discovered Siouxsie Sioux or seen any other Goth girls, she-this girl who I never saw again and whose name I never learned- became the standard of beauty that I aspired to for years.

"Oh, sorry," I said as I moved out of her way.

She got excited when she saw the album in my hand. "Oh cool, they have it! That's what I'm here for, too. Oh, I hope they have another copy."

My heart sank. What if this is the only copy? I'll have to give it to her. She deserves it more. And she'll be so grateful...

"Yes! They have one more copy! I guess we're the lucky ones who get them!" For a moment I wondered who she meant by "us." And then I realized that she was including me, that I was part of "us" to her. She smiled at me and I wanted to follow her home and ask her to teach me how to be like her.

"I just love The Cure, don't you?" she asked. Was she testing me? Did she suspect that this townie with her ripped, faded jeans and Skid Row shirt was a poseur?

"Oh, yeah," I said. "They're great." I could feel my cheeks burning. I wanted so much to act cool and pretend that I had been listening to them for years. But for some reason, I didn't want to lie to her. "I mean… I just started listening to them…"

"Oh, you'll love them. They're my favorite band. Get 'Pornography' too. It's their best." She turned and started walking toward the counter to pay. Then she stopped and turned as though she had just thought of something. "And if you like that, check out Bauhaus." She thought for a moment. "And Siouxsie and the Banshees."

"Thanks." I said and then before I could stop myself I blurted out "By the way, I think you're really pretty."

"Aw, thank you," she said, looking down shyly and brushing a strand of hair behind her ear. Then she went up front and paid and left. I picked up a copy of "Pornography" slightly embarrassed by the title. I'd have to hide that one from my mom. I went and looked through the "B" section until I found Bauhaus, not knowing how to spell it. I decided to wait until I had more money to get some of their records. I looked for "Susie and the Banshees" but couldn't find it. I didn't figure out how that one was spelled until much later.

I often wonder what happened to that girl. What adventures life took her on. Sometimes I think of her as a dark fairy godmother, sent to me at just the right time, to steer me in the direction my life was supposed to take. Maybe I just don't want to think of her as the middle-aged soccer mom that she probably became. After I paid for my records, Elise and I left. We stopped at a drugstore on the way home and I bought my first bottle of black hair dye.

# TRACK 6: NO ONE LIVES FOREVER

By now, the audience is getting restless and bored. *This isn't what we came for. Nostalgia and music and hair dye. Where's the blood? We were promised blood!*

Well, first of all, this is my story. If you want me to tell it, it's going to be on my terms. You need to know my history. You need to know where I came from and how I got from there to here. I'm not some faceless victim to be slaughtered for your titillation. Nor was Elise. Nor was Joey (poor Joey, I haven't even told you about him yet, and here I am rushing ahead). You have to know these things. They are important.

Besides, any Horror writer will tell you that you have to make the reader care about the characters before horrible things start happening to them. It has more impact that way. Only the hacks populate their stories with one-dimensional stereotypes who exist only to become victims. Here's a secret: those writers- the ones who don't take the time to make the victims in their stories into real human beings- their sympathies lie with the killer. They write their stories so they can live vicariously through their villains. They want you to cheer when the Prom Queen gets decapitated. And some of you do.

But, this isn't that kind of story. This isn't murder porn. I wasn't the sex-crazed prom queen. Joey wasn't captain of the football team. Elise wasn't a spoiled princess. We weren't stereotypes or symbols. And we didn't deserve what happened to us.

Very well, if you want some blood...

We weren't the first. It was no secret that there had been a series of murders in our little town. Over a dozen teenagers, mostly girls, had gone missing over the previous decade. Some of them were probably just runaways. But others most definitely were not. Many disappeared under very mysterious circumstances. One girl, Caroline Davis, two years older than me, had gone missing a year before. Her body was found a few months later in a wooded area outside of town. Eventually her father was arrested for her murder. The police were hopeful that they would be able to tie him to the other disappearances. But there was no evidence connecting him to any of the others.

After days of being questioned by the police and conferring with his pastor, he finally broke down and admitted he had been molesting Caroline for years. He had killed her accidentally, he said, one night when he got drunk and tried to rape her. She fought back and things got out of hand. He hanged himself in his cell that night. His body was cremated after the local newspaper received several anonymous letters, vowing to exhume his corpse and burn it, if he were allowed to be buried in the town cemetery. Caroline's murder didn't fit the pattern of the others. Her body was dumped far from where she was killed, whereas the other victims were left where the killer found them. And Caroline wasn't mutilated like the others. Still, people held out the hope that her father was the killer and that at least no one else would be victimized.

But then Kristin Forester never came home from her closing shift at the Tastee Freez. Her car was found the next day in a farmer's field, her body a few yards away. Mutilated like the previous victims. The papers never said in what way they were mutilated. But we heard things. There were whispers, rumors. He cuts their hearts out. He cuts their private parts out and takes them home with him. He cuts them in half. It was always just "he" or "him". Everyone under the age of twenty in our town had heard about The Huntsman, but we rarely spoke his name. People knew who you were talking about by the tone of your voice or the context of what you said.

No one knew where the stories started, but everyone heard it from someone at a sleepover or around a campfire. It was a ghost story that you told your friends to scare them in the dark, no different from Bloody Mary or the hook hanging from the car door. Except this version was local and was based in reality. Someone would tell you that they heard it from their older brother or a worldly cousin, but no one knew who *they* had heard it from. It was just a part of our local adolescent folklore that there was a mysterious killer named The Huntsman preying on teenagers and killing them in horrific ways.

But, we didn't care about any of that. Even though we knew people who knew some of the dead and knew the places they were killed, it still seemed distant to us. Even though our high school put up a glass case with pictures and memorials to the students who were lost, those things wouldn't happen to us. Besides, the display case also contained memorials to kids who died from diseases and in car accidents. Some kids just don't make it to adulthood. All of their deaths seemed connected, like parts of one big tragedy. We believed that all of their deaths were caused by some extraordinary circumstance or some bad decision they made. And that belief made us feel safe. The stories of the deaths were still distant and only slightly more real than stories in books or horror movies. They gave us a thrill and a jolt of uneasy excitement. Our parents certainly worried more than most small town parents. But they still didn't believe that anything really bad would happen to us. We were good kids, even if we dressed funny and listened to scary music. We never got into real trouble. Things like that didn't happen to good kids. Our virtue would protect us.

So, we didn't exactly lie to our parents. We just didn't really tell them where we were going. And they didn't really ask. It's hard to believe now, but back then parents didn't track their children's every movement. Once you had your driver's license, you were expected to have a certain measure of independence. Still, our parents would never have approved of us driving the two hours to Richmond on a school night. Much less to see a heavy metal concert. We knew we would get in trouble when we came back late, but we didn't care. Seeing this concert, seeing Danzig live, was a matter of great importance and urgency. Nothing in my adult life has ever compelled me the way seeing a band compelled me as a teenager. The music was what we lived for, and everything else was a chore that had to be endured.

The push and pull of being a teenager is that your brain is wired to seek excitement and new experiences. And your parents are torn between wanting you to experience the world and wanting to protect you from it. The more your parents see something as dangerous, the more attractive it is to you. As an adult, I'm horrified at the thought of us going out by ourselves, knowing that there was a murderer at large. What happened seems so inevitable and avoidable. But that's just hindsight. Cause and effect seem so much more obvious as an adult. I can also remember my teenage brain telling me that sitting at home watching "Who's The Boss?" when one of my favorite bands is playing two hours away, was a fate worth risking my life to avoid.

"Ya know, maybe we shouldn't go." We were hanging out on one of the picnic tables outside of the cafeteria during lunch break, surreptitiously passing a cigarette between us. It was early November, and the air was starting to turn chill at night, but the afternoon sun was still warm. The doubts had begun to nag at me. Thinking about how much trouble we would actually get in, I was starting to have second thoughts.

"What are you, a fucking pussy?" Elise responded in her typical demure manner. "God, we never do anything fun anymore. We didn't even do shit on Halloween."

This wasn't entirely true. We had taken Elise's little sister, Courtney out trick-or-treating and then we had watched "Nightmare On Elm Street" (with Elise's running commentary about all the dirty things she would like to do to Johnny Depp) and snuck a couple of swigs of her Mom's vodka. But it was a school night, so we couldn't stay up too late. And we were too old to trick-or-treat ourselves.

"Every day is Halloween," I responded, trying my best to sound spooky.

"Okay, fine, Morticia. If all you want out of life is to be the spookiest little girl in Bumfuck, Virginia and pass up the chance to actually go out and do something fun, you can stay home and do your homework. Or finger yourself to your Andrew Eldritch poster, or whatever you do when I'm not around."

Joey let out an embarrassed giggle. He hadn't been involved in the conversation, had been preoccupied with watching the door to the cafeteria in case a teacher came out, ready to ditch the cigarette quickly if he had to. But the mention of anything sexual always caught his attention. I think that was part of the reason he hung out with us. And I know that Elise said things like that to get a reaction out of him. And to embarrass me, of course.

I rolled my eyes, hoping that the gesture conveyed annoyance instead of anger or embarrassment. "I just didn't want you guys to get in trouble."

Elise scoffed. "Oh, please. My mom will have a cow, but deep down she'll be kinda proud of me. And Joey's folks probably won't even notice he's gone."

Joey looked away and took a drag off the cigarette. I thought Elise was a bitch for saying that, even though we all knew it was true. He didn't talk about his home life much. He didn't have to. We knew. We had overheard the things our parents whispered about his parents. They're drunks. His father had been in jail and didn't have a job. His mother was crazy. He never invited us over to his house and we understood why.

"You know you're just worried that Mommy won't think you're her perfect little Cassandra anymore. You never get in real trouble, anyway. She'll ground you for a week and then she'll change her mind after two days like she always does."

"That's not true," I said. Although it sort of was.

"Come on," she said. "I dare yoooouuu…" She was trying to do her Peter Murphy impression, but it always came out sounding more like The Count from Sesame Street.

"Fine, we'll go. I don't give a shit."

Looking back, I can't believe how easily I was goaded into doing things I didn't want to do back then. But, I suppose no teenager is immune to the "what are you, chicken?" reverse psychology. And to an extent, that was just the dynamic of my relationship with Elise. She the tempter, brave and adventurous. Me, reluctant and wary. We fell into these roles early on and stuck to them. Truthfully, I was more adventurous than I pretended to be, and she was more cautious than she let on. But we played our roles, and we kept each other in balance.

We made plans to meet at five o'clock at Cicero's Pizza, our favorite hang out. It was our favorite because it was the only place in town with video games and a juke box with something other than country. The restaurant was run by first generation Italian Americans who moved to our little town from Brooklyn, to raise their kids in a safe small town. I took for granted how lucky we were to have real New York-style pizza in the rural South. Their pizza is, to this day, the benchmark that I measure all pizza against. Going to Cicero's, loading up on greasy pepperoni and sodas (Cheerwine for me, root beer for Joey, and Diet Coke for Elise, who was already inheriting her mother's obsession with weight loss) was a part of our ritual every time we hung out in the evening.

Joey was already there when I came in a little before five, playing Galaga. AC/DC was playing on the jukebox. Joey had probably selected that, not because he especially liked AC/DC, but because it was the heaviest of the bands he had to choose from. I can still remember the smell of Cicero's. The feel of the hard plastic chairs. The front window would have still been plastered with the Jack-o'-lantern coloring sheets that they gave to kids to fill in every October. I always loved coloring those, and I loved seeing that younger kids still did.

I started to say Joey's name and then stopped myself. I just stood and watched him play. He seemed so excited, so into the game. I realized that when he was playing video games was the only time I ever saw him genuinely enthusiastic. He loved listening to music, but it seemed to serve only to make him more intense and brooding. Video games made him come alive. I think because they were the only place where he had a measure of control. Where he could make things happen, instead of just having things happen to him. I wish he had been able to see what video games would be like in the decades to come.

It occurred to me as I watched him that the reason he was already there before either of us was because he hadn't gone home. He had just come straight from school and waited for us. I went over and stood next to him and watched him play.

He glanced over at me quickly, and then returned his attention to the game.

"You look nice," he said. He gave me compliments like that from time to time. I think he was trying to flirt with me, but he could never look at me after the words came out.

"Thanks. I just barely had time to re-dye my hair and redo my makeup."

He nodded quickly and concentrated on his game.

I heard the front door swing open and Elise came bustling in, slightly out of breath from the walk from home. "You guys order yet?"

"No," I said. "Just got here."

"Well, just get me the usual." She headed towards the bathrooms at the back of the restaurant.

I went up to the counter to order for all of us. I'd like to say that I remember everything we said while we ate. That I remember how every bite tasted. But, I don't. It was like a hundred other times we ate there, no indication that anything was different. We ate, we drank our sodas, we talked about the same dumb things we always talked about. Then, when we were done, we piled out. The sky was getting dark, and the air had started to take on a chill. We climbed into my car. I started the engine up and put a tape in the player and we pulled away into the night.

# 8

She awoke early, after a restless night. The sun was not yet up, and there was a pale blue glow around the edges of her blackout curtain. She knew from the anxious flutter in her stomach that it was futile to try to get back to sleep. She would have to get up, do something for a couple of hours, and hope that exhaustion would overtake her sometime in the afternoon. She got up and dressed in the darkness. Knee brace, then jeans, faded from black to charcoal gray. She pulled a baggy hoodie over her head and pulled on the battered combat boots she wore whenever she left the house. She slipped quietly out the front door and stood in the darkness of the porch. The wind blew gently and a light mist fell. In the distance, she could hear the ocean's roar. There was nowhere to go but to the beach.

Foulweather Bay didn't have sidewalks or even streets wide enough to walk down. There were walking paths interlaced between neighborhoods, but the paved roads were meant for the sole purpose of driving to and from one's house. Widening the streets, or paving them better, or making the town easier to get around, would only have encouraged more tourists to visit. And that was the last thing most of the town's residents wanted. Their fervent desire was to keep the town small and quiet, and most of them had the money to ensure that it happened.

She walked along the narrow path between well-tended yards. Sporadic pools of light filtered through massive rhododendron bushes that glowed like embers in the predawn. A few blocks down, a narrower path led down to the beach. It was unlit, a tunnel of impenetrable darkness. This is stupid, she thought. People who have received death threats should not go walking down unlighted paths alone, as a general rule. What if he's down there? Waiting for me?

She laughed at herself. Right, makes perfect sense. He's just waiting on this dark path a quarter of a mile from my house, on the off chance that I'll wake up early and decide to go for a stroll. That's not how this works. He'll come for me, but he'll come to my house. Walk right up on the porch and knock on the door. Or kick it down.

Her logical mind knew this was true, but cold fear still gripped her as she walked into the darkness of the path. Her heart beat faster, and she quickened her pace as much as the knee brace would allow. She held her breath for the fifty feet until the woods opened up and she was on the open sand. She had to walk slowly in the loose sand at the top of the rise. Her doctors had said that walking on the sand was good for her, would strengthen the muscles in her legs. But she had to be very careful. One wrong step and her leg would twist under her and give out. When she got closer to the water's edge, where the sand was packed down by high tide, it was easier.

The wind blew harder and colder here. Damp and salty. She put her hood up and stuck her hands in her pockets and walked along the shore just beyond the tide's reach. She loved the ocean because its eternal indifference made her feel that any problem she might have in life was insignificant and ridiculous. The sky in the east was just beginning to glow a pale grey. The hills rose sharply up from the sea and were blanketed with thick forest that looked like a painting done by a child who was determined to use every shade of green in his palette. The trees that grew closer to the water were all bent, blown by the relentless wind until they submitted and curved with it. The sand was littered with driftwood and the long bullwhip kelp that always made her think of alien tentacles, so unlike anything she had seen on the beaches of the Atlantic. The hollowed out shells of crabs lay everywhere, the remnants of a seagull feast. As she walked along, she periodically looked behind her, feeling that she was being followed. But she was alone.

He could come up behind me out here and I wouldn't even hear him over the surf, she thought.

She had walked less than one hundred yards before her leg began to burn with the exertion and she sat in the sand and stared out at the waves. In the universe of her books, the ocean was vast and unknowable. No one had ever sailed across it. Mariners sailed away for years at a time and never found another shore, giving up and turning back when their supplies ran low. Or simply sailing on and on, never to return. If one stood on the shore at daybreak, stars could be seen falling from the sky and drowning in the distant water beyond the horizon. And on stormy nights you could hear the voices of the dead drifting in on the sound of the waves. The people in her books believed that when you die your soul goes to live at the bottom of the ocean. It was traditional to say to the dying a phrase which roughly translated to "We will meet again, beneath the waves."

She sat on the sand and closed her eyes and listened, thinking maybe she might hear Elise or Joey. Telling her they forgave her? No, that was selfish. She had no right to expect their forgiveness. But maybe they would tell her what it was like living at the bottom of the ocean. Did Elise live in a castle made of coral? Did Joey have a mermaid harem? Did they fly through the water amongst schools of fish, vibrant and colorful as tropical birds?

She heard a voice, faint and ghostly. It's cold here, it said. It's cold and dark and I'm alone. The voice repeated this over and over until she jerked her head up and realized that she had dozed off there in the sand, her head rested on her crossed arms. She began to cry, because she couldn't shake the image of Elise lost in the darkness of the ocean floor, trying to find her way back to land. She looked down the beach and saw a figure walking toward her. Panic filled her for a moment. He's here, he found me. I can run, but I won't be fast enough. I can scream, but no one will hear me. For a brief moment she saw herself living the nightmare of being chased through deep sand, unable to will your legs to move faster.

She stood stiffly and with difficulty and looked back to the figure approaching her and saw a smaller figure moving faster, back and forth to the water's edge. A dog. She laughed. Of course, it was just one of her neighbors out taking his dog for a morning walk on the beach. Murderers don't bring dogs with them to the beach.

She didn't feel foolish, though. That fear had been real. It stayed with her as she walked back up the beach, up the path, and along the street back to her house. She sat at her desk, still wearing the hoodie, still chilled by the ocean breeze.

She took the envelope of pictures from the drawer, spread them out on the desktop. She hadn't wanted to look at them before, couldn't bear the pain and nostalgia she knew they would bring. But now she was numb and just wanted to feel something. They were out of order, a picture of her at seventeen in full Goth regalia followed by the ten-year-old with a ponytail and a Care Bears shirt (Grumpy Bear, of course). She and Elise on a hideous seventies-vintage couch looking annoyed that their photo was being taken. Joey head-banging to "Master of Puppets." These were the only photos she had from the old days. She cherished them, but only looked at them every few years.

The one at the bottom was the most recent. It was one of the last photos taken of her before college, and she had no copies of any pictures taken since this one. She didn't even keep prints of the author photos taken for her book jackets. She hadn't looked at this last photo in years, stopping and putting the pile back in the envelope before she got to it.

The picture was of her, taken from the side and slightly behind. She was looking down. It wasn't black and white, but the colors were so washed out that it almost seemed to be. And of course she was wearing only black and her skin was even paler than usual after the months spent in the hospital and in her bedroom. The photo only showed her from the shoulders up, so the crutches weren't in frame. She was wearing a long sleeve shirt that went up to her neck and heavy makeup, so the scars and bandages weren't visible. She was framed in the center of the photo, so the photo didn't show what she was looking down at.

She never knew what had possessed her mother to take a picture at a time like that. It was bad enough that her mother had insisted over and over that they go to the cemetery. That she visit their graves. That it was important, that it would give her closure. She had gone to the funerals, but had been unable to bear to see them lowered into the ground. Her mother had felt strongly that seeing where they were buried was an important part of the grieving process. Her mother had even tried humor to persuade her, saying "I thought you liked hanging out in cemeteries." The joke had no doubt sounded a lot funnier in her head.

Finally she relented, agreed to go see their graves. Get some of that closure that her mother kept promising her. On a cold, bright day in early January they went out together. Her mother asked if she wanted to take her car, try to drive a little. She just shook her head, hadn't driven in months and in fact wouldn't drive again for years. While she was at college, she took the bus to and from classes. Her classmates would have thought she was a complete hick if she had told them how excited she was by the concept of public transportation. Her mother would ask, during her weekly phonecalls, what Cassandra wanted done with the car, just sitting there in the driveway. Finally, she had said simply "sell it." Her mother said okay and a couple weeks later sent her a check for the $500 she had gotten for it.

Her mother drove them to the cemetery, and she looked out the window and didn't say anything. On the way there she saw a couple of boys she knew from school walking their bikes along the road and she looked away from the window down at the floorboard and hoped they hadn't seen her.

The sunlight there in that flat field was overbearing. That kind of hard brightness that you only get in the wintertime. The wind was frigid and bit at her cheeks. They went to Joey's grave first, just a patch of bare dirt marked with a typewritten piece of paper in a plastic holder. His parents hadn't even scraped together enough money for a tombstone. Years later when she started making money from writing she had one made for him, in case some relatives came to visit him. She never saw it herself.

As they walked to Elise's grave, she felt as though she was emptying out of herself, going hollow. Floating above the ground. I'm a ghost, she thought. I'm a ghost haunting someone else's grave.

When her mother snapped that photo of her, she was looking down at Elise's stone. And all she could think was, why couldn't it have been me? Why can't it be me, too? If her mother had been able to see her thoughts imprinted on that sheet of cheap photo paper, all she would see was a longing to rejoin her friend. To follow her into whatever darkness she had gone into. A longing to die more powerful than anything she had ever felt. They drove home, and she went wordlessly to her bedroom and lay down on the bed and cried silently for what seemed like hours. She barely left her bedroom, or even her bed, for the next week.

When she reemerged, her mother gave her the photo. She felt violated that her mother had taken it. But she cherished that photo throughout the years and would take it out whenever she had a desire to feel that pain again. Poke at the scar with a fingernail, probe the rotting tooth with her tongue. Whenever she wanted to feel like a worthless piece of shit that didn't deserve to survive when her friends had died.

Now, a middle-aged woman, sleep-deprived and cold, sitting at a desk a continent and a lifetime away from the girl she had been in that photo. It was stupid, she told herself. To still mourn friends from childhood. We probably would have grown apart, wouldn't even talk anymore. They would just be pictures on my Facebook feed by now. But none of us had a chance to grow at all, to move on.

Sure, it's stupid, but so am I. I'm a stupid old woman who can't get over something that happened thirty years ago. That still lives in the fairy tales of her youth. That can't have normal adult relationships. A man wants to kill me, because we're both stuck in this stupid childhood ghost story. I should save him the trouble.

She kept an antique dagger on her desk, ostensibly as a letter opener. She took it up now, pulled up her sleeve, and pressed the tip to her wrist. Pressed harder and harder, felt the sting as it tried to puncture her skin. She drew it along her arm and it left a faint red line. She drew it across the old faded scars on her forearms, remembering those old feelings. Cutting herself had always felt, not good exactly, but right somehow. It felt bad, but it was satisfying. She wanted so much to just press down, open herself up. Then do the other arm. Lean back in her chair and wait for sleep to come. Her hands began to shake, and she suddenly felt dumb and melodramatic.

I can't die without feeding the cat first anyway, she laughed to herself. She put the dagger back on the desk and went and laid down in bed with her clothes still on. She shivered under the blankets for an hour before exhaustion overtook her.

# TRACK 7: IN THE FLAT FIELD

And that brings us back to where we started, the foreshadowing we opened our tale with. We were driving down the road in my VW Rabbit. We were listening to the mixtape that one of the clerks at Dark Planet had made for me. He had a crush on me and enjoyed nurturing my burgeoning musical taste. I played it until it was warped and eventually lost it, but to this day I can still remember the order of the songs. "Sonny's Burning" had just ended and Bauhaus was up next. After that was a song by a mostly forgotten band called Screams For Tina.

We were on the road out of town that led to the highway, which would take us the hour and a half to Richmond. I can close my eyes and still see the buildings we passed on the way. The school, the library, the gas station. The wealthy neighborhood where we didn't know anyone, but still went trick-or-treating every year, because they gave out full size candy bars. Through the tunnel beneath the train tracks. Over the river and through the woods. Past the cemetery and then the highway stretching into the dark.

"What the fuck is going on over there?" Elise brought me out of my trance of watching the lines on the road, and I noticed the lights in the cemetery. Red and blue flashes lit up the darkness, strobing off of the newer stones not yet dulled by age. I slowed to try to get a better look, but all I could see were the dark outlines of police cars and men walking around in alternating shades of blue and red.

"Jesus," I said. "I've never seen that many cops. Do we even have that many?"

"Must be the Sheriff. State troopers." Joey didn't say much, but when he did, it was usually to convey useful information. "Must be something really bad, to call them."

"I wanna see," Elise said. "I wanna see what it is. Maybe it's grave-robbers." She was bouncing in her seat like a kid on her way to see Santa Claus. "Or maybe it's zombies. 'They're coming to get you, Cassandra.'"

"Joey's right. Whatever it is, it's probably pretty bad. It's not something we want to see." Even so, I had pulled to a stop under one of the trees at the edge of the graveyard and was straining to get some vague image of what was going on over there in the dark. "Besides, they're not going to just let us go in and look around."

Elise sat sullenly for a few moments and then brightened up. Her face widened into that mischievous grin that I knew meant that she was about to suggest something that would get us hurt or in trouble. "The House! You can see the whole cemetery from The House!"

"No. No way," I said. "I'm not going in there at night. And before you ask, hell yeah I'm chicken." Joey didn't say anything, but I could hear him shift around in the back seat.

I'm doing my best to show and not tell, but a little background about The House is in order. The House by The Cemetery, or simply The House, was an old Victorian on a small rise above the graveyard. Abandoned since before we were born, it was a legendary presence in the minds of all children in our town. It was haunted, of course. Ghastly murders had been committed there years before. The last scion of a once wealthy family, a reclusive spinster, had lived out her last days there, growing more and more insane until... and a dozen other stories, none of them with any basis in fact.

We were forbidden to go into the house. So, naturally, we all did. It was a dare, a test of bravery, a rite of passage. Our parents' concerns about us exploring the house centered on tetanus and lead paint and asbestos and broken legs from falls. But, to us it was just them trying to keep us from experiencing something exciting.

The floorboards sagged, and the wallpaper peeled. Piles of plaster littered the floor. The walls were spray-painted with crude, unimaginative graffiti: pentagrams and random curse words and racial slurs. Barely recognizable pictograms of pot leaves and penises. Empty beer cans were strewn everywhere. When we were little, the thought of those older kids who were so fearless that they could sit and drink beer in an obviously haunted house awed us. And years later, when we became those teens, we were still scared. But the beer helped make us less afraid.

In the previous year, we had stopped even going to the house to drink. Partially because of the murders and rumors that The Hunstman lived in The House. But mostly because it was well known that The House had become a shelter for transients (who we still called "hobos" in those days) from the nearby railroad tracks. At first they kept to themselves and only slept there at night. But then a few started showing up when teenagers were there drinking and asking for beer. And then we heard a rumor that one of them had exposed himself to one of the girls and suddenly it seemed that our parents might have had a point about avoiding The House.

But now Elise was suggesting that we sneak in and spy on whatever crime had attracted every cop in a twenty-mile radius.

"Okay, fine." Elise had opened her door and was getting out. "If you two Girl Scouts wanna stay here and braid each other's hair, go ahead. I wanna see." She slammed the door, and Joey and I sat in the dark.

"I should just leave her here." I said.

Joey gave a non-committal grunt from the backseat. "Yeah, I guess. It's close enough, she can walk home."

"We're gonna be late for the show if we don't leave soon." I realized then that I had been unconsciously shifting the car into first gear and then into neutral and back again. Elise had disappeared into the darkness along the overgrown road that skirted the cemetery and led to The House. My hand hovered on the gearshift for a moment, and then I shoved it into first, started to let off the clutch and then pushed it back in. I set the parking brake and shut off the engine.

"I'll go get her." I said "You can stay here."

"Fuck that. I'm not gonna stay here by myself and have to explain to the cops what I'm doing here."

And that was it. We piled out of the car and followed the path that Elise had taken along the cemetery. We could barely see the ground in front of us in the dim illumination that filtered through the trees from the lone security light in the parking lot. The red and blue flashes were faint and distant, blocked by the gentle slope of the cemetery. We could hear murmuring voices of police officers, but couldn't make out anything they were saying. They seemed hushed and almost reverent, mourners at this bizarre late night funeral.

We hurried along the path, trying to keep our breath hushed as it steamed out of us. I wish I had a flashlight, I thought. I wish I had breadcrumbs to leave a trail so we can find our way home. The House loomed ahead of us, a dark shadow against the sky. It's not made of gingerbread, I thought. Even in the dark I can tell that.

If this were a movie, Elise would have jumped out of the

dark to scare us. A jump scare sets the audience on edge and makes them more susceptible to the real horror that follows. Am I giving too much away? Yes, there is real horror to follow, but I suppose you already knew that. At any rate, this isn't a movie and Elise didn't jump out and scare us. She was standing on the sagging, deathtrap front porch, waiting for us like it was her own house and we were late for a play date.

"Bout time you wusses caught up. C'mon." And she turned and pushed aside the front door that had hung from a single hinge as long as we could remember. That last hinge must have been made of impressive stuff, because it refused to let go.

We had been in The House in daylight and we had been there with groups of people as the sun went down. But, to be there in full dark, just the three of us, was something else entirely. I tried to tell myself that the fear I felt was grownup and reasonable fear. The fear of falling through a rotten floorboard and breaking an ankle. The fear of stumbling over a sleeping transient who might not take kindly to having his slumber interrupted. The very real possibility that one of the dozen police officers less than a hundred yards away from us would catch us there and arrest us for trespassing. But, deep down, I knew that there was a more childish fear underlying it all. The fear of the dark, the fear of unknown places, the fear of things that hide in the shadows and wait to do us harm. There are no ghosts. There are no monsters. Of course not, everyone knows that. You tell yourself that, but your brain doesn't always listen.

Elise marched confidently across the front hall and up the creaking staircase. I thought at the time that she was utterly fearless. But I know now that there are people who are motivated and energized by their fear and Elise was one of those people. She thrived off of the rush of fear. I followed inexorably behind her. My mind raced with things I should be saying, trying to convince her to turn around and come back to the car. But I couldn't form them into words. I knew it was pointless. And besides, the fear was becoming a rush for me as well. I enjoyed being pulled along in Elise's wake. I always put up a struggle at first, but eventually I gave in and just went along for the ride. For his part, Joey had taken being in The House as an opportunity to light a joint and followed silently along behind us, taking hits from time to time.

We came to the top of the stairs and crossed the upper hallway to one of the tall windows that fronted on the cemetery. Peering out we could see the parking lot jammed with police cars, all flashing lights in different rhythms. There seemed to be even more of them than before.

"Jesus." I said. "What the hell happened down there?"

For the first time we could see the single non-police vehicle parked over at the edge of the lot. It looked vaguely familiar.

"Whose car is that? I know I've seen it at school." They didn't know. Joey squinted at it and tried to place it in his mind.

"Yeah," he said. "I've seen it before. Some jock's car. I've seen it over by the football field, where they all park."

There were flashlights playing around amongst the tombstones, but from that window we couldn't see what they were lighting up. One of the gnarled, ancient trees in the front yard partially obscured our view. Elise moved down the hall to the next window, and we followed. We could see a little better there. But we could still only make out police officers in a circle, shining their lights on something on the ground.

"Still can't see what it is." Elise said in frustration. "Come on."

"We can't go in there!" My voice come out louder than I wanted it to and for a second I thought that surely one of the police officers would hear. Of course none of them could hear me through thick old window glass and hundreds of feet of night air. And they were too focused on whatever was on the ground to notice, anyway. Elise was heading for the door of the corner bedroom, a room none of us ever went into. It was an even more forbidden portion of an already forbidden house. Ostensibly, we avoided it because the floor had collapsed in one corner and there was a hole just big enough for a person to fall through. But, because of this danger, the room had become a de facto sanctum for the "bad kids." Teenagers who did things that we were unsure of, but that we knew were beyond the pale for us. Drugs harder than beer and pot. Sex. There were even rumors that some boys experimented with satanic rituals. In my twenties I knew some practicing Satanists and I know now that those were just kids who didn't know what they were doing and just wanted to feel dangerous. But at the time it felt like a real threat. Elise would not be denied, though.

"We can't see shit from here. We'll be able to see better from the windows in there. I didn't come all this way to watch a bunch of redneck cops play flashlight tag."

"We're gonna miss the show if we don't go soon. Did you forget about the show?" It seemed almost that she had. Like she hadn't even thought about the show since she first saw the lights in the cemetery.

"You're right," she said. "So we better pull our thumbs out of our asses and go see what's down there, so we can leave." She turned and went through the door into the bedroom. I looked at Joey, who had crushed out the joint and was looking out the window as though it was just the sunset out there. No help, as usual. He would just go along with whatever Elise and I decided to do.

I sighed. "I suppose we might as well go take a look. We've come this far."

"Okay," Joey said. I might as well have just decided to go

to Burger King instead of Tastee Freez, for all the emotion he showed.

The bedroom had an unsettlingly unclean smell on top of The House's general smell of age and decay. It smelled like a place where animals slept. I couldn't quite place it, but I detected definite notes of rancid beer. Smoke, both cigarette and pot. A pungent scent that I, at the time, only vaguely associated with sex. And indeed there was a filthy, stained mattress on the floor, recklessly close to the gaping hole in the corner. My expectations of evidence of Satanism were also fulfilled; there was an inverted pentagram spray painted on the wall and burned down black candles on the floor. Probably just dumb teenagers playing around and then having a circlejerk afterward. But, I didn't know that at the time. Fear and revulsion filled me like ice water being poured from my stomach to my groin.

Elise was crouched at the front window, peering excitedly like a peepshow voyeur. Breathlessly, we walked up behind her and looked over her shoulders. I wanted nothing more than to just get this over with and leave. I didn't care anymore what was down in the cemetery. I just wanted to be back in the car and driving. To the show, back home. I didn't care, just somewhere else. We could see now what the policemen were looking at. An unmistakably human shape, laying between two graves and covered in a white sheet. It was lit by their flashlights, but the men were setting up work lights on stands and running extension cords back to the parking lot.

They switched on the work lights and the cemetery was suddenly bathed in light as bright as day. We squinted against it, our eyes adjusted to the dark. A man in slacks, a dress shirt and windbreaker, the only man not wearing a police uniform, walked into the circle of light and gave a few quick directives to the officers. A few of the men looked away or shuffled off into the dark as the plainclothes man crouched and pulled the sheet back.

From where we were, we could see her perfectly, there on the ground, all lit up like a Christmas pageant angel. My memory has probably added more details than I could actually make out at the time, but I remember it with a flashbulb, spotlight clarity. We didn't recognize her at the time because she was crimson with blood from head to toe. Her clothes were torn off of her. Joey turned away. Did he avert his eyes as much from her nakedness as from the violence done to her? Maybe, although there was nothing remotely sexual about it. Still, you could see that she had been beautiful. Whoever did this to her couldn't deface her completely.

Her right breast was still incongruously pristine, though smeared with blood. The left side of her chest, though, was obliterated as though hacked at by an inept butcher. Elise stared in reverent awe. Joey had turned from the window and was making a noise that was somewhere between hyperventilating and sobbing. I wondered if that was the first naked girl he had ever seen. At the time, I thought that was a stupid thing for me to think about. But, now I know that it probably was his first and I feel bad for him. Something that he had built up in his mind and thought about for years and that should have been beautiful, made grotesque and horrific. It probably would have caused him sexual dysfunction in later life. But, as it turns out, that wouldn't ever be an issue.

We didn't know who she was at the time. We only knew that she was our age. And whether she was someone we got along with or someone who bullied us, she was still one of us. We felt her loss, and we felt regret that we had come to gaze upon the atrocity that had been inflicted on her.

Are you happy now, I thought. Happy that you got to see it? Elise wasn't happy, though. There were tears in her eyes as she turned from the window and walked slowly out of the bedroom. I hate myself now for that brief moment when I was mad at her.

I don't remember walking back to the car. I don't remember if we were careful leaving the house, looking out for tripping hazards and holes in the floor. I don't remember if we were quiet as we walked along beside the cemetery or if we didn't care if the cops heard us, knew that they were too preoccupied to pay us any mind. I just remember driving away. I wasn't sure where I was going. I just wanted to get away from there. Joey was hunched in the back seat, like he was trying to fold himself up and hide. Elise stared silently out the window.

"You missed the highway," she said. At that point we were already miles past the on-ramp. I had completely forgotten that once, a long long time ago, we had been going to a concert.

# 9

Over eight thousand words in two days. Cassandra had always been a consistent thousand-words-a-day writer. A book every two years. Six months for a first draft, with long periods off to think and contemplate and build the world in her head. Revisions and rewrites and multiple drafts until the story was perfect; or until she was completely exhausted. But now the words flowed from her. A stream of consciousness, where her previous works were meticulously crafted prose poems. For those two days she barely got up from her desk and lived inside her head, in her memories of 1990. But, after writing about Mary's murder in the cemetery, she came crashing into the present and found herself unable to think about it anymore.

She looked up from her monitor after staring at those last words she had typed and wondered how long her phone had been vibrating. She got up and retrieved it from its perch on the shelf by the door, where it stayed plugged in whenever she was home. Almost no one knew her number, so it wasn't unusual for her to go for more than a week without a call. Seven missed calls. All from Anthony. She dialed him back.

"Cass? Christ, I thought you were dead or something."

"I was working."

"You don't even check your email anymore? I've been trying to contact you. I finally gave up and decided to drive out there to make sure you were still alive. I'm about a half hour away."

"I'm fine. You don't need to check up on me. Go home and go to bed."

"Excuse me? Fuck that, I already gave up a good night's sleep and drove over an hour to talk to you. And if nothing else, you need to make me some coffee and let me use your bathroom before I turn around and drive my ass back to Portland."

"Okay, okay. I'll see you when you get here."

She hung up and went to the kitchen to start a pot of coffee. It was dark outside the windows and the wind off the ocean was making the wind chimes sing on the back patio. While the water was heating, she realized that she couldn't remember if she had eaten anything that day. She opened a can of soup and poured it into a pot, and set it on the burner. She heard a car pull up out front and a door shut. The security light on the front porch came on as Anthony unlatched the gate and came up the front walk. It wouldn't be anyone else but him. But still she looked through the peephole in the front door before opening it for him.

"I brought your mail in. You shouldn't let it pile up like that. It makes it look like you're not home and someone might take it as an invitation to break in." He handed her the stack of envelopes and she sorted through them absently, tossing the junk mail into the recycling bin.

"No one's gonna break in here. Most of the people who live around here have dinner at four and are in bed asleep by seven."

"It's not people around here I'm worried about. Did you read any of the emails I sent you yet?"

"No, I haven't been online. I told you I was working." She stirred her soup and then poured him a cup of coffee. "Black?"

"Yes, I am. Thanks for noticing."

"Har har, that joke never gets old." She looked at him expectantly.

"I'll take a little sugar. I just remembered how strong your coffee is."

She handed him the cup and started to look through the rest of her mail. There was an envelope from her lawyer, a man that she had only met in person once. Probably some papers she needed to sign. There was also a letter with her name and address hand written and no return address. She recognized the handwriting. Anthony was saying something, but she couldn't hear it. This letter was postmarked San Luis Obispo, California. That was where she had gone to college.

"Cass! You're not even listening to me."

She looked at Anthony blankly for a moment and thought about what he had said. His statement was definitely true. She had not been listening to him. She tried to think of what she was supposed to do with that information. And the letter. What was she supposed to do with that, again? Another piece of information forced its way into her brain just then. This one slightly more urgent, the fact that her soup was starting to boil over and sizzle on the burner. That was an easy one. She knew exactly how to deal with that piece of information. She decided not to worry about those other two pieces of information until she had decisively dealt with the matter of getting the soup off of the stove and into a bowl. After a moment's reflection, she dismissed the idea of pouring it into a bowl as being more trouble than it was worth. She set the pan on a hot pad on the table and got a spoon and sat down to wait for the soup to be cool enough to eat without sustaining third-degree burns. In the meantime, she could take care of whatever those other two things were.

"You're absolutely right," she said. "I was not listening to you." She stirred her soup absently and looked at the letter and wondered what on earth she was supposed to do with that thing?

"Cass. Listen to me. There was a murder. In Dark Hollow Falls."

She stopped stirring. "I don't think I want to know about that. Do I?"

"Probably not. But you should be aware of it, even if you don't want to be." She looked at him like a little girl waiting for her parents to tell her why her dog didn't come home from the vet.

"Cass. It was a copycat. A teenage girl. Mutilated. Her heart cut out. They didn't find her for a few days, but she went missing last Tuesday. The day that letter you got was postmarked."

"That letter I got. Oh, that thing. It's funny, because I was just about to tell you about this." She held up the new letter to show him. He looked at the post mark.

"San Luis," he said. She nodded.

He got out his phone. "I'm calling the police."

"You won't get anyone at this time of night," she said. "Not around here. Not unless you call 911. And I don't think getting a letter in the mail constitutes an emergency. "

"I'm calling the State Police. I spoke to an investigator after the last letter. He said to call him if you got another one. He was the one who told me about the murder in Virginia, but I didn't know about this new letter when I spoke to him." The investigator must have answered then, because Anthony turned his attention away from her and began talking into his phone.

The soup was cool enough to eat now. It wasn't bad for canned. She hadn't even looked at the label before pouring it into the pot and she was pleasantly surprised to find that it was Italian wedding. One of her favorites. She didn't listen to what Anthony said. She already knew all of it. It's all so tedious, she thought. And cliched too. If I were writing this book, I would never do something as predictable as a copycat killer.

But, it's not a book, is it? No, this is actually happening. She ran her hand along the wood of the table. I am here, she thought. This table is real. The soup is real. Jonas is sleeping in his little bed by the heat vent and Anthony is here and he's talking on the phone about that letter. I should open that letter and see what it says. And then the fear came, a tight little lump of ice pressing against the bottom of her stomach. The fear she had been trying to avoid. It was here now.

Anthony was finishing up his conversation and sat down across the table from her. He took a sip of the coffee and winced a little.

"Well," she asked. "What did your friend from the State Police have to say?"

"He agrees with your assessment, that it does not constitute an emergency. He said he would call the local Sheriff and have them drive by the house a few times throughout the night. And he'll stop by tomorrow to look at the new letter. Their opinion is that the first letter was so vague that it can't really be classified as a threat. Might just be an obsessed fan who has an awkward way of showing their devotion. What does the new letter say, by the way?"

"I don't know. I haven't gotten around to opening it yet."

He looked at her incredulously. She ripped the envelope open and pulled out a single piece of paper. Like the previous letter, it contained a single handwritten phrase. She chuckled.

"Okay, so what does this one say? More song lyrics?" She handed him the paper, and he read it: "'The scarlet thing in you'. Let me guess, Peter Murphy again?"

"Yep," she said. "Same album, even."

"Maybe it's from someone you knew in college. This one was sent from San Luis. And you said that was your favorite album in college. Maybe it's from that guy who bought the album for you. Maybe he's still pining away."

"I highly doubt it. And he doesn't live in San Luis anymore. He wrote me a letter once through Sutton House. He lives in Denver, I think. He barely remembered me, but his teenage daughter likes my books, so he was trying to earn some 'cool dad' points by proving to her that he used to know me. So I wrote her a letter and sent her a signed book. I was nice and didn't tell her about the band. Or all the times her dad tried to get me to sleep with him."

"Well, whoever is sending these letters, we have to treat them as a threat until we know otherwise. I'll call Sutton House in the morning and discuss the possibility of getting you some kind of security here. I don't suppose there's any chance I could talk you into going back to Portland and staying with me tonight, is there?"

"No. You're overreacting. We don't even know if these letters are threats. And this one was sent from San Luis Obispo. That's a long way from here."

"Cass, you're not thinking clearly. San Luis is, what, a fourteen hour drive from here? And that letter was sent two days ago. The person who sent them could be here right now."

"Doing what? Walking on the beach, looking for shells? Staying at the Bed and Breakfast down the road? Is he gonna get up in the morning and write me some more song titles over tea and scones?"

"Well, at any rate, if you won't go back with me, I'm staying here tonight. That's not a request."

"Oh, fun! A sleepover! Can I paint your nails? Can we play truth or dare?" Anthony just looked at her.

"Okay fine," she said. "But you have to sleep on the couch.

And you don't get to complain if Jonas decides to sleep on you."

"That's fine."

"And I'm not making you breakfast."

"That's fine."

"In fact, you get up way earlier than I do, so you should have coffee ready for me when I get up."

"Fine. Although I doubt mine will be strong enough for you."

"And I'll probably be up late. I want to write some more. You'll need to go to another room and not bother me. I can't be bothered when I'm working."

"That's fine. So," he went on, trying not to sound too eager. "you want to get back to the writing? It's going well then?"

"Oh, it's just making me perfectly miserable, darling. It's a little like being stuck at your best friends' funerals for days and not being able to leave. Thanks for asking."

"If you don't think it's healthy for you... I mean, if it's making things worse..."

"Oh, don't give me that bullshit. It's too late for that. The genie is thoroughly out of the bottle. The wound is ripped open and there's nothing to do now but sew it shut. Ha! As you can see, I am in full novelist mode now. Verily, the shitty metaphors simply flow out of me."

She took the dishes and rinsed them out in the sink.

"Okay," she said. "Make yourself scarce. I have a few more memories to get down on paper before I can sleep."

"Okay. I'll go in the bathroom and call Bart and say good-night to him, if that won't bother you too much."

"No, that's fine," she said. "Poor Bart, he's probably still waiting up for you to come home. What's that..." she had started to ask a question, but stopped herself.

"What's that, what?"

"I don't know. I think I was going to ask you what it's like to have someone waiting for you to come home. But, I guess that's something you can't really answer."

"Do you get lonely?"

"No. I used to, I guess. Lonely isn't really the right word for it. It's more a longing for something that doesn't really exist. And that you know you can't ever have. I miss human companionship the way I miss having full use of my leg."

Anthony nodded and started for the door to the bathroom. She stood there, watching him. He stopped and turned.

"Was there something else you wanted to ask?"

"Well," she said. "There is something I've always wondered about you guys."

"Yes?"

"How do you decide who gets to be the little spoon?"

"We take turns," he said. "Now get to work."

She wrote for several more hours until she had trouble focusing her eyes on the screen. It was a great feeling when she was in the groove of what she was writing and she would type late into the night, losing track of time, until she was too exhausted to do anything but get up and brush her teeth and collapse into bed. She closed out of her word processing program and got up and stretched. Only then did she realize how sore her back was and how badly she had to pee.

And then she remembered Anthony. It had been two hours. Could he still be in the bathroom talking on the phone? She opened the bathroom door to find him sitting on the floor with his back against the wall and his legs straight out in front of him. His hands were clasped together in his lap. His phone and glasses were set neatly on the sink and he had a rolled-up towel propped behind his head. She never ceased to be amazed at his ability to sleep anywhere, under any conditions.

"Hey, sleeping beauty," she said, gently shaking his foot. "You can move to the couch now. I'm calling it a night."

He leaned forward and opened his eyes as though he had merely been resting them for a few seconds.

"Okay," he said. "If you're ready."

He got up, not showing any sign of being stiff or sore. No sign that two hours spent on a cold tile floor had affected him at all. For a second, a thought crossed her mind that maybe she should let him share her bed. That he deserved a soft warm bed instead of her broken down old couch. And that maybe it might be nice to have a warm body in bed with her, just to see what it was like. She loved him, of course. It wasn't romantic. More familial than anything. But still, to have someone you loved sleeping next to you. That would be nice, wouldn't it? Then she thought of the idea of rolling over, stretching in her sleep and feeling human skin there in the darkness. The idea repulsed her.

"It's pretty late," he said. "The writing must be going well. Do you feel like telling me anything about it?"

"No," she said. "As a matter of fact, I don't. You know perfectly well I don't talk about any of my books while I'm still working on them."

"I know. I thought maybe this one was different since it's autobiographical. And because you're digging up a lot of things you haven't thought about in a long time. I thought maybe you might need to talk about it."

"No thanks. I can go back to the shrink if I need that. Now, get out so I can get ready for bed."

# TRACK 8: BOYS DON'T CRY

We had stopped in the parking lot of the high school. I don't remember driving there. I just wanted to drive away from the cemetery and I didn't think about where I was going and then I started to head out of town and then I saw the lights in the school parking lot and I turned in there. I turned off the engine and shut off the headlights and we sat in the dark of the parking lot and no one said anything and it was so quiet. I ran my hand along the soft plastic of the steering wheel. I remember how it felt. Isn't that weird? All these years later, everything that happened that night, and I still distinctly remember how it felt running my hand back and forth along the steering wheel.

"We should go home," I said. No one responded. Elise was staring down at her hands, folded in her lap. She might have been crying. I don't know.

Finally she said "I don't want to go home. I just want to keep driving. I don't want to close my eyes, because whenever I close my eyes I see her. Do you know who she was?"

"Is," said Joey.

I shook my head. "I couldn't recognize her, the way she was."

"We shouldn't have seen that," said Joey. It shocked me. I had never heard him say anything so definitive. "We shouldn't have been there."

I started the car back up. I turned on the headlights. The dim light from the dashboard and the weak stream of warm air out of the heater vents was comforting. I realized I had been scared, sitting there in the dark. With the engine running, the car was once again a little bubble of safety. My chariot to take me through the dark night. My suit of tin armor on wheels. I drove to the entrance of the parking lot and sat there, wondering where we were supposed to be going.

"Should we go to the concert?" I asked. The car's little engine chugged and idled up and down. It always did that when it was sitting still. I tapped the accelerator, because I had figured out that doing that made the engine calm down and run smoother.

Elise shook her head. "I can't imagine going and listening to music and trying to have a good time."

"We should go home." Joey was full of surprises tonight. Another definitive statement. And a desire to go home. Things had to be really bad to make Joey want to go back to where his family was.

I pulled out and turned back toward town. I tried to think of something to say. I felt like I needed to fill the silence, but there were no words for what we were all feeling. I thought about putting music on. I didn't know if that would be wrong somehow. I tried to think only about driving, but my mind kept going back to the girl in the cemetery. She was one of us. Probably went to our school.

Everyone's going to be crying tomorrow. We'll know tomorrow who she was. They'll tell us, they'll break it to us gently, in that way that adults have of telling kids about awful things. Something came back to me that I hadn't thought about in years. The time in fifth grade when they let all of us kids take a break from school work to watch TV in class.

We were so excited, because we never got to watch TV at school. And it was the launch of a space shuttle. We were witnessing history. Plus, one of the astronauts was a pretty young school teacher. She could have been one of our teachers. She looked like them. We sat and watched in awed silence, and before we even knew something was wrong, the shuttle exploded. I remember my teacher Mrs. Stern muttering "Oh my God." Mrs. Stern was a very conservative Southern Baptist, and we were forbidden from taking the Lord's name in vain in class. Her shocking act of blasphemy scared me. She slowly walked over and switched off the TV and sat down behind her desk, and began to pray. A little girl next to me started crying.

Is that what it will be like tomorrow, I wondered. The Challenger disaster was my only frame of reference for this kind of tragedy. I was trying to mentally prepare myself for what was coming. How should I act? We'll have to pretend like it's a surprise. We can't let anyone know that we were there, and that we had seen her. I was thinking about all of this, and Elise was saying something. She said it again, but it still didn't register. Then she said it a third time and this time she was almost yelling and I realized she was saying "stop sign!"

I slammed on the brakes and the wheels locked and the little car skidded on squealing tires and stopped with the nose a few inches into the intersection. Joey lurched forward and slammed into the back of my seat and grunted, "fuck!" A pickup truck went through the intersection in front of us, horn blaring. The car had stalled, because in my panic, I had hit the brake pedal without stepping on the clutch.

"Are you guys alright?" I asked.

"Were you fucking sleeping or something?" Elise was pissed.

"Oh god, I'm sorry. I was distracted, okay?" I turned to

look at Joey. He was leaning back in his seat, rubbing his forehead. "Are you okay?" I asked.

"Swell. I'm probably going to have a bruise."

Headlights pulled up behind us. The driver immediately honked their horn at us, so I turned around to start the car. I turned the key, and the engine cranked and cranked but wouldn't start. The driver behind me honked their horn again. "I'm trying. Jesus." I kept turning the key, but nothing happened. So, I rolled down the window and waved for the car behind me to go around. They gunned their engine and sped around us and through the intersection. The driver flipped me off as he went past.

"Fucking assholes in this town," I said, as I tried to crank the ignition again. The sound was becoming strained, and I knew from experience that if I kept trying, it would just run the battery down. I turned the key off.

"You've gotta be fucking kidding me," said Elise.

"I'm sorry, alright? It does this sometimes. It gets flooded or something. We just have to wait awhile and then it should start up."

"We should get it out of the road," said Joey. "Let me out, I'll push."

Elise got out and pulled the seat forward so he could climb out. He got behind the car and started pushing and Elise pushed on the door frame while I held in the clutch and cranked the steering wheel as hard to the right as I could. It was a light car, and it didn't take much to get it moving. It coasted a couple of feet and then it was all the way off the pavement and I put on the brakes. We had all grown up poor, so pushing a stalled car off of the road was nothing new to any of us. Joey climbed back into the rear seat and Elise got back in and shut her door. There was nothing to do but wait.

The intersection we were at was miles from town, in the middle of farmers' fields. It was dark, no streetlights. We could see the lights of houses far out across the fields, but they were all at least a half a mile away. A few cars went by, but no one stopped to ask if we needed help. We even saw a few police cars, but none of them stopped either. On a normal night they would have stopped, either to see if we needed help or to hassle us, depending on what mood the cop was in. But they were too busy tonight to pay us any mind.

"I'm sorry you guys," I said. I'm not sure what I was apologizing for. Everything, I guess.

It was getting cold in the car. I tried to start it again. Please, I thought. Please start, so I can turn on your comforting lights and your heater and maybe even play some music. We can be home in fifteen minutes. I turned the key, and the starter cranked, but the engine didn't catch. I pumped the gas, but it didn't help. The starter began to strain and get slower and I knew that the battery was getting too weak, so I had to give up. I put my head down on the wheel and cried a little.

"Well," said Elise. "I guess we're walking."

It's such a cliche isn't it? The car that won't start. I even mentioned earlier how it would stall sometimes. Foreshadowing. Chekhov's Volkswagen. That's how it happened, though. Of course, in stories like this we want some underlying moral, some reason that the Bad Thing happens to The Protagonists. Some thing that they did wrong that brought retribution from the universe. We made choices that led us into our fate, but ultimately The Bad Thing happened because I had an old car that I got for free and it needed carburetor work. None of it would happen today. One of us would just get out their phone and call someone to come pick us up and we would sit and play games or watch videos until someone came. But we were miles from a payphone and we hadn't seen a car in a while, so we got out, locked up the car and started walking back towards town.

Elise was wearing the leather biker jacket that she had

inherited from her cousin when he sold his motorcycle.. He was one speeding ticket away from losing his license. I had on the trench coat that I wore constantly from September through March. We both had on combat boots. Ironically, Goth wardrobes are well suited for walking along country roads in the cold. Joey was only wearing his denim jacket, so he must have been cold, but he never let on. We walked along for a couple hundred yards of uneven gravel and scattered puddles, trying not to twist an ankle or trip over a beer bottle in the dark. We saw headlights approaching.

"Do you think they'll stop?" I asked.

"We'll be lucky if they don't shoot us," Joey said.

We waved our hands as they drove past, but they just blew their horn and yelled something unintelligible at us.

"Okay," said Elise. "Next car that comes by, pull your tits out so they stop."

"Yeah, sure. Why don't you pull yours out?"

"Because mine are nicer than yours. We want them to give us a ride, not rape us."

Joey had walked on ahead. He turned on us suddenly and said, "Will you two please shut the fuck up and walk faster?" and then started walking ahead of us even faster than before. Elise and I just looked at each other. We were too stunned to be mad. We had never seen him angry about anything. And we had certainly never known him to not be interested in us talking about our breasts. We walked on in silence for the next fifteen minutes.

My toes were cold. My feet hurt. I tried not to focus on that, but if you're walking and your feet are uncomfortable, it's hard to think of anything else. I tried to think about what I would do when I got home. I would draw a hot bath and just soak in it for an hour. I would make a cup of hot chocolate. I hoped we had hot chocolate at home. I decided not to think about that anymore because it just made my current situation more miserable. But, when I stopped thinking about that, my mind drifted back to the girl in the cemetery. So I went back to focusing on how much my feet hurt. I walked along, looking down at the ground just in front of me, trying to spot things I might trip over in the darkness. I was a few feet from Joey when I realized he had stopped walking.

"There's a house over there," he said. "Their lights are on."

We were still a few miles from town, but there were a few more houses, not just farmhouses out in the middle of fields. The house Joey was looking at was up a small hill from the road, and it was the first one we had seen that looked like anyone was awake. People go to bed early in farm country. The house was small and looked old. But, it wasn't run down. It looked nice. It looked like a place where one of our friends might live. There might be someone our age in there, watching TV or listening to music.

"We should go see if they'll let us use their phone," Joey said.

"You gonna call *your* parents?" Elise asked.

"No," said Joey. "We're gonna call one of your moms. They'll come get us. My parents would just yell at me for bothering them and hang up on me."

"I think we should just keep walking," I said. Why the hell did I say that? The last thing I wanted was to keep walking. "I don't want to get in trouble."

Elise looked at me in disbelief. "What, you think if you walk home, she just won't notice that you didn't bring the car with you? Were you planning on walking back out here tomorrow and pushing it home?"

"I don't know," I said. "I thought... I don't know... we could call your mom and her boyfriend could come get it running for us or something."

"Well," said Elise. "For one thing, he's working tonight. And even if he wasn't, it would be after midnight before we got the car home, anyway. Face it, you're just going to have to admit to mommy that you were driving to Richmond, and the car broke down and take your punishment like a big girl. You can keep walking if you want, we're gonna go see if these people will let us use their phone."

I felt like crying and I didn't know why. "I don't want to sit in some stranger's house while we wait for a ride."

"What strangers?" she said. "There's like two thousand people in this town. Whoever lives in this house, I'm sure one of us knows them. But whatever, we can sit on the porch while we wait. It's still better than walking."

It wasn't though. I didn't know why, but walking seemed better. Walking was miserable, but at least we were alone and we weren't getting yelled at for lying about where we were going and leaving the car broken down out in the middle of nowhere. I couldn't explain all of that to them, and they were already walking up the driveway to the house, anyway. So I followed.

We walked up the cement steps to a closed-in porch. There was a Jack-o'-lantern on the steps, starting to get mushy, and paper skeletons and witches taped to the front door. The house was all lit up and there was an old pickup truck in the drive-way, but there was no sound from inside. Elise knocked on the screen door of the porch. No answer. She opened the screen door, and we walked across the porch and she knocked on the door to the house. It swung open. It hadn't been latched.

The living room was lit up, but we didn't see anyone inside. It looked like the interior of hundreds of houses we had been in. It had probably last been redecorated sometime in the seventies. Everything was in shades of brown and beige. Clunky wooden furniture and a black iron woodstove in front of a brick mantle. A deer head mounted on the wall. It reminded me of my grandparents' house.

Elise knocked on the door frame again and called out,

"Hello?" No answer. "Is anyone home? We just need to use your phone."

There was still no answer. Elise pushed the door the rest of the way open and peeked her head inside. I wanted to stop her. "Look," she said. We peeked in at what she was looking at. There was a phone on an end table just inside the door. It was the same beige rotary phone that almost everyone in town still had. Push button phones were still a novelty. Most people still just had the one that you rented from the phone company. I knew what she was thinking.

"No," I said. "You can't go in there."

"Watch me. It's right there. I'll call my mom and tell her where we are and she'll come get us. It'll take two minutes. It won't even be long distance so they'll never even know." She went in and picked up the receiver.

I turned to Joey. "I'm not going to wait here until her mom comes. What if these people come home and find us here?" The sound of my voice surprised me. I sounded like a scared little girl. I sounded almost hysterical. I don't know why it scared me so much. Joey was as calm as ever.

"It's fine," he said. "He'll just wait along the road. We can start walking towards town again and she'll meet us along the way."

Elise was dialing the phone. Actually dialing it. We still say "dial the phone" and I wonder if younger people understand why we say that. Well, you see kids, it's because phones used to have a plastic dial on the front and you would put your finger in the hole for each number and turn the dial and then let it rotate back. Then go to the next number and do it again. It took almost a minute to dial someone's number back then and if you screwed up, you had to hang up and start all over. She turned the dial and let it click-click-click back into position three times, and then stopped.

"Shit," she said. "I can't remember my own goddamn

phone number. I haven't had to call it in years." The phone started to make that noise, that noise that I don't know the name for. It was like a busy signal, but it was the noise that phones made if you didn't finish dialing. She pressed down the little plastic tabs on the cradle and looked at me. "Christ, Cassy. What's my fucking number?"

"I don't know," I said. "I can't say it, I have to dial it." Back in the days before cell phones, we had to remember people's phone numbers. One of the ways we made it easier was that we didn't consciously remember all of them. The ones we dialed all the time were just involuntary muscle memory. Our fingers remembered the pattern to dial them, but if we had to write them out or say them out loud, we would draw a blank. Elise's number was like that for me. I had called it at least five times a week since I was ten. If you put an old rotary phone in front of me today, my fingers could probably still dial the number without me even thinking about it. I decided there was no point in arguing anymore. She had already gone into this stranger's house and picked up their phone. So if someone came home we would all be in trouble. We would just have to hope that they felt sorry for us. Or better yet, make the call fast and get the hell out before they knew we were there.

I walked into the house.

# TRACK 9: THE BOY WITH THE THORN IN HIS SIDE

Poor Joey. I wish I could stop thinking of him as "Poor Joey" but that's who he always is in my memory. I always think of him as just being along for the ride. If Elise and I had told him we were going to drive to New York City to buy crack, he probably would have tagged along with us. I know I'm doing him a disservice by thinking of him as just tagging along, but that's how it's set in my mind. Elise and I chose our own path that led us into Hell, but Joey was just pulled in our wake. He wouldn't have gone out that night if we hadn't had the idea. He just didn't want to be left out. Because he had a crush on me? Did he have a crush on me? I think so. Or maybe, like most teenage boys, he was just happy to have any attention from the opposite sex.

God, this is so predictable. I'm denying him his agency. And I'm also casting Elise and myself in the role of temptress. Twin Eves causing his fall from grace. Stealing his innocence. Leading him to ruin. My therapist would call this internalized misogyny. And maybe she's right. Maybe society teaches girls to accept responsibility for the choices that boys make. Raises us to be little masochists.

I did tease him a little. Sing to him "Joey, honey…" just to watch him blush. I don't know if he had even heard that song or if he thought it was just something I made up. I think he enjoyed it, even though it embarrassed him. I hope he did. He was such a sad, broken boy and he deserved some happiness.

"They don't love me," he told me once. He said it so matter-of-factly. He wasn't complaining, just stating. I knew who he meant. He didn't talk about his family much. They were just a fact of life, like a flat tire or getting rained on while walking home. Complaining about it wouldn't do any good, so why bother? Except in families like his, complaining made it worse. Acting like it bothered you made it worse. So, become passive. Accept your lot in life.

I had a recurring fantasy during my twenties that Joey and I were married. I didn't understand it, I had never had romantic feelings for him. But whenever my anxiety would get really bad and the memories of that night came rushing back, I found myself pushing those thoughts away and fantasizing that he and I lived in marital bliss. It was a coping mechanism, what my Psych professor called "maladaptive day-dreaming." Finally I realized that I was living out my desire to give him the happiness that he deserved but never had. Elise and I were at least happy most of the time before that night. Joey never was. He was lonely and sad. Elise never got to be an adult. I never got to be anything but a hollow shell of an adult. Joey never even got to be a kid. My fantasies of being married to him were childish wish fulfillment and a way for me to deal with the guilt of having the life he never had.

I've replayed what happened next a million times in my head, but it still never quite makes sense. It seems more like a dream I once had than something that actually happened to me. I walked into the room. Joey stayed on the porch. I don't know why. Maybe he was looking out for another car pulling in the driveway. Maybe he had a bad feeling about coming inside. I took the receiver from Elise and she took her finger off the cradle. I started to dial her number and then I heard a noise behind me. Elise and I turned and saw that the door was closed. Why was it closed? Did Joey close it to play a prank on us? No, he wasn't that type. I thought that maybe the home-owners had come home, and he panicked and shut the door so they wouldn't see us inside.

I called his name. He didn't answer. Elise was annoyed. She grabbed the knob and tried to open it, but it wouldn't budge. It was locked, but that didn't make sense because we were inside. Why would it be locked from the outside? There was a noise out on the porch. I can't describe the noise, it was just the sound of movement. Certain noises always make you feel uneasy. Because they just sound wrong. Too urgent, too emphatic. Then there was a heavy thud of something dropping on the boards of the porch, and I knew something was very wrong. Elise turned to me.

"What the hell is going on?"

I didn't know. I went over to the door and tried the knob myself. You just have to see for yourself, right? Have to know that you're not being the victim of a prank. Or maybe Elise was just doing it wrong? Pushing when she should have been pulling. Or maybe you had to lift up on the knob to get it to turn. My bedroom door was like that for almost a year until my dad got around to rehanging it. Maybe that's all it was. But the door wouldn't budge. I pushed, pulled, lifted. It was locked tight. I knocked and called out Joey's name. Nothing.

You know those dreams where, no matter how much you try to make yourself move, everything is in slow motion? Your limbs weigh a ton and every step feels like trying to walk against the current of a river. You try to yell, but your voice comes out as muffled gibberish. Time seemed to slow down. I turned around slowly and saw Elise. She was standing in the middle of the room, staring blankly at the door. As though she couldn't process what was happening. How the door could suddenly close on us and be locked from the outside. Why Joey wasn't answering. That something was very wrong. I said her name softly. She barely seemed to notice that I was there.

A couple of years ago, I watched a documentary about mass shootings. One of the people interviewed was a former police officer who now trains people on surviving active shooter situations. Something he said stuck with me. He said that the reason most people are killed in mass shootings is because they refuse to accept what's happening until it's too late. It's too incongruous with their perception of reality, so they tell themselves that it's a bad joke. It's just fireworks.

We should have run out the back door of the house when we had a chance. Or broke a window and crawled through. But our minds wouldn't accept that in a moment we had gone from being together on the porch to being separated from Joey and locked inside a stranger's house. We believed that the regular order of the universe still existed and so we were frozen in indecision.

And then it was too late. I heard a sound of movement coming from the back of the house, and I looked into the darkness of the hallway beyond the light of the living room lamp. A man was walking towards us out of the darkness. And I couldn't see his face. He was wearing some sort of garment that looked like a parka, but made of leather. And it had a hood, and he had the hood pulled down over his face. It looked like something a character in a Medieval Fantasy would wear. It was so odd. Why would someone wear a hood over their face inside at night? I thought I should say something.

"We… just needed to use the phone. The door was open and…."

The man showed no sign that he had even heard me. He walked on slowly, almost casually. As he came into the room, I looked down at his hand for the first time and I noticed that he was holding a knife. It was huge. His hand hung at his side, and the blade extended well below his knee. He turned his wrist and I could see the broad side of the blade and I could see that it had blood on it.

"Oh my god," I said. Elise followed my eyes to the blade, and I heard her gasp.

She went back to the door and started to pull harder on the knob and jam her shoulder into it. "Joey!" she yelled. "Open the door, Joey!" She stopped for a moment, like she was deciding what to do next, and then she raised her foot and jammed the heel of her boot into the wood of the door. The noise was shockingly loud and the wood of the old door made a cracking sound, but it barely budged. The force of her kick recoiled into her and she staggered back, almost falling into me. As she regained her balance and put her foot down, she grimaced in pain.

The man in the hood lunged for us, swinging the knife wildly like a sword. Elise put her hand up, and the blade struck just below her pinky, dug in and stuck. She shrieked in pain and anger and pulled her hand back. She held it in her other hand against her stomach and blood spurted down the front of her jeans. I grabbed the closet thing to me, the phone, picked it up and swung it towards the man's head as hard as I could. It struck the end of its cord just as it hit the side of his head, so it didn't have much force. But it was enough to slow him down for a second. But only for a second. And then he started laughing. And then I heard his voice for the first time. I still hear it in my head to this day. It was little more than a whisper, but it was filled with more hate and anger than any other voice I've ever heard.

"I'm going to enjoy cutting you little cunts up."

We circled around behind him, keeping him in our sight. We backed up towards the hallway. Elise had wrapped her hand in the hem of her shirt to try to stop the bleeding, but it had soaked through and dripped on the floor. He lunged towards us, leading with the knife. We turned and ran, stumbling down the hall, through a door at the other end. It was the kitchen. Without even thinking, I slammed the door shut just as his bulk collided with it. The frame around the knob cracked and splintered, but it held. The door had an old-fashioned bolt lock, and I pushed it shut. He tried to open it. Then I heard his foot steps go back down the hall, a moment of hesitation and then I heard him running and the sound of him colliding with the door again, loud as a gunshot. The wood splintered and the bolt lock bent. He would get through the next time.

Elise had found a kitchen towel to wrap her hand. It instantly turned red, but it didn't soak through. Her shirt and the front of her jeans were soaked with black blood. I looked desperately around to find a weapon, but there was nothing. No knives out on the counter, no skillet to use as a club. We had to keep running.

Ramming the door twice must have slowed the man down a little, but after a moment I could hear him walking back down the hall and then running towards the door again. We went out the back door of the kitchen. It led into a narrow pantry that had probably been the back porch before being closed in for extra storage. The walls were lined with shelves full of canned goods, boxes of laundry soap, a big old kettle. There was a door to the outside. I grabbed the doorknob just as I heard the door to the kitchen break open. The knob didn't budge. It was locked. Every door in that house must have locked from both sides. To lock people in.

Elise was taking rapid shallow breaths and I don't know if she was scared or just in pain. Was I scared? I don't know. Fear isn't the right word for it. It was more of a primal state of self preservation. I didn't panic, though. To this day I don't know how I didn't, but in the ten seconds that it took him to cross the kitchen and come through the door to the pantry, I thought very clearly about what our options were. Breaking down the door would take too long. There was a small window to the outside that was just big enough for us to crawl through. I knew it would be locked. And I knew I would have to slow him down.

As he appeared around the corner, he stopped to look at us. Savor the fact that he had us cornered. I took advantage of his hesitation and ran toward him. He didn't expect that, and he froze. As I ran past the shelves, I grabbed blindly at the first thing my hand went to. It was a big Mason jar, and I swung it as hard as I could at his face. It connected the way the phone should have, if the cord hadn't stopped it. He lowered his head slightly at the last second, and it hit his hooded forehead. I didn't want to risk missing, so I followed through and the jar exploded in my hand. Glass and lima beans flew everywhere, and the shards sliced my fingers. A small one lodged in my palm. The impact staggered him and brought him to his knees. He dropped the knife, and it clattered on the floor. I should have grabbed it. I wish I could scream back through the years to myself to grab the knife and end it there. But I still hadn't accepted what was really happening. I wasn't thinking clearly. My only thought was escape. Get out of the house, as though we would somehow be safe once we were outside.

The pain in my hand sent me into a blind fury. I ran and jammed my shoulder and elbow through the pane of the window. It broke and my momentum almost carried me through and out onto the ground. I used my forearm to knock as much of the glass out of the frame as possible. My other hand was cut now. And there was a sharp pain in my eye like a grit of sand at the beach. I wouldn't find out until much later that a sliver of glass had lodged in that eye and my vision would never fully recover. At the time, I just knew we had to get out. Elise was already bleeding, so I guess I figured it was my turn. She was right behind me, so I went through first. I must have missed a piece of glass because I felt a thin razor-like cut opening on my side as I crawled through. I tumbled to the cold ground outside. Elise crawled through after me and I helped her down. We ran back around the front of the house. I didn't hear the man follow us, so he must have been knocked out, or at least dazed. But I knew it wouldn't last long.

As we came around the corner and the front porch came into view, I looked desperately for Joey. Had he left? Run away? Then I saw him. He was sitting on the front steps with his elbows on his knees, head down, like he had fallen asleep waiting for a friend to come over and play. He was just sitting there while all of this was going on. I hissed his name. He didn't respond. Was he asleep? In shock?

I ran over to snap him out of it and when I touched his shoulder, he slumped back against the steps and there was a dark stain down the front of him and his eyes were wide open but they didn't see anything. There was a gaping wound, like a second mouth, where his throat used to be. His head lolled back on what was left of his neck, and his open eyes stared skyward. Elise started crying behind me, because she saw. I'm glad it was dark, so I couldn't see better. We said words, but I can't remember what. I was crying, but there wasn't time. We had to go. We had to leave him there and run. We ran down the driveway and back along the road toward town. Hoping we would see a car.

Poor Joey.

# 10

Cassandra awoke the next morning, just before noon. She slept in sweatpants and an AFI t-shirt that was old enough to vote. It was faded and had a few holes, but she had been wearing it every night for over ten years and would have felt odd sleeping without it. Ritual is important. Familiarity is a weapon against chaos.

She got out of bed slowly and carefully. Her bad knee was always stiff and sore and untrustworthy in the morning. She got her cane from beside the bed. She rarely bothered putting on the brace until she had used the bathroom and bathed and dressed for the day. She put on her bathrobe and walked out into the living room and was about to ask Anthony why he didn't have coffee waiting for her. There was a man on her couch. A white man, in his forties, with short-cropped blond hair. He wore khaki pants and a white polo shirt. She had never seen him before. For a moment she thought, Oh! Here he is, my mysterious letter writer, come for a visit. The man looked up at her and nodded.

"Morning," he said.

Cassandra blinked and stared at him. Anthony spoke from the kitchen.

"Good morning, sleepyhead. I heard you moving around so I'm getting some coffee going for you."

"Lovely," she said. "By the way, did you happen to notice that there's a person in my living room?"

Anthony came out of the kitchen. "Sorry. Introductions are in order. Cassandra, this is Detective Conley from the State Police."

"Oh, fantastic," she said. "You know how much I enjoy having strangers in my house. Especially surprise strangers."

Conley stood up. "I apologize if I startled you. Mr. Lucas called me about the letters you've been receiving. Foulweather Bay is a little off the beaten path and I don't get up this way much. I happened to be in the area this morning, so I stopped by."

"I'm sorry," she said. "I don't mean to be rude. I just don't have visitors very often. And I'm not a morning person."

Conley chuckled. "Me neither. Unfortunately I chose a line of work that requires me to pretend to be one."

Cassandra smiled. In spite of herself, Conley's manner put her at ease. But then, cops are trained to put people at ease, aren't they?

"Well," she said. "If you'll excuse me I have to go powder my nose."

She went into the bathroom, used the toilet, brushed her teeth and splashed water on her face. She thought about combing her hair, but decided that was overly ambitious. When she went back out, Anthony and Detective Conley were sitting on the couch and there was a cup of coffee waiting for her on the end table. She sat in her favorite chair and took a sip.

"How did I do?" asked Anthony.

"Well, you make coffee like a little old lady. But it's not bad. You're improving. Did you offer our guest some?"

"He did," said Conley. "And I turned him down. I'm trying

136

to cut back. But, on second thought, it does smell pretty good. If it's not too much trouble…"

"No, I'll get you a cup." Anthony said.

Conley was looking at the letters. "So, you get one letter sent from the town in Virginia where you grew up and on the same day it was postmarked a young woman is murdered in the same manner as… well. And then a second letter from the town in California where you went to college."

Anthony came back in and handed him a cup of coffee. Conley went on.

"Do you want to me to tell her?"

Anthony shook his head. "Cassandra," he said. "Conley just found out this morning that there was a second murder. In San Luis Obispo."

"Oh my god," Cassandra said, putting her head in her hand. "Don't tell me. She… because of course it's a 'she' right? She had her heart cut out, and the murder happened the same day my second letter was sent. Right?"

They didn't say anything, because they didn't have to.

"Okay," she said. "What do I do now? Some psycho is killing people. Because he's obsessed with the psycho who killed my friends. And he's sending me letters every time he does it because… I don't know why. Because he thinks I'll be impressed? Or to let me know he's gonna kill me next?"

"Well," said Conley. "Let's just stick with what we know. We strongly suspect that these letters were sent by the killer. But, we don't know for sure. And we don't know for sure what the intent behind the letters is. The good news, if it can be called that, is that because of the letters we can connect the two murders. Two murders on opposite ends of the country. It might have taken a while for everyone to connect the dots. But, because the connection was made, the FBI is involved. They take over whenever a murderer goes across state lines. The bad news is, the FBI hasn't shown much interest in these letters.

They asked me to take them as evidence, just in case they can connect them to the murderer in the future. But, they mostly blew me off. Do you mind if I take them?"

"I don't know," she said. "I might need them."

"Need them for what? If you don't mind me asking. Something to do with your writing?"

"No," she said. "It's hard to explain, but objects retain some of the energy of the people who possessed them. I might need some of that energy. To use it against him. But, I need to find out if he's a threat to me first."

Conley nodded. "Is this a, uh, Wiccan thing? I noticed some of your books and the Tarot cards."

Anthony said "Yes, Ms. Watson is a former practitioner of witchcraft and her beliefs are..."

"Anthony!" Cassandra cut him off sharply. "Do not speak for me. And do not try to 'explain' me to people."

He was speechless for a moment. "I'm sorry," he said. "You're right. Would you, uh, like some more coffee? It looks like your cup is empty."

Cassandra told herself not to be angry at Anthony. Usually she wouldn't tolerate him talking about her like she wasn't there. But she knew that he had a deep-seated sense of unease around cops and he was probably just over-compensating for that.

"That would be lovely, thank you. And yes, Detective. As my assistant, who apparently forgot that I am capable of speaking for myself, started to say: I am a practitioner of witchcraft. I've lapsed a bit in the last few years and I know now that was an error. I took its power for granted and I need to start respecting it again."

Anthony brought the coffee pot in and refilled Cassandra's cup. He offered Conley some, but he shook his head.

"No, I've definitely had enough. Any more and I'll be awake til midnight. My wife is Wiccan." Cassandra couldn't conceal the surprise on her face. Conley just chuckled. "People are always surprised. We're kind of an odd couple, I guess. I used to get teased a bit by the other cops for being married to 'a witch.' They keep it pretty good natured though. After I made it clear to them what would happen if they didn't keep it good natured. Mostly they just call us Darrin and Samantha, now. I don't really believe in it and I'll admit I thought it was a little weird when I was younger. But then I realized that if the woman I love believes in it and it's important and powerful to her, then it is important to me too. I respect her, so I respect the things she believes."

"You might be the most enlightened cop I've ever met," said Anthony.

"Thanks," said Conley. "Just don't let it get around, okay? My wife owns a little bookstore down in Newport. She stocks metaphysical books, crystals, some fiction. If you ever make it down that way, she'd be thrilled if you stopped in. In fact, I'm not really supposed to discuss my cases with her, but with your permission I'd like to tell her I met you. She was a big fan of your books when we met back in college."

"Of course," she said. "By all means give her my regards."

"Well," he said. "I suppose there's no harm in you keeping the letters. I don't know that I could really enter them as evidence, anyway. Because I don't know what they're evidence of. Mr. Lucas told me that the lines written on them have some personal significance for you. But I don't think we could even plausibly consider them threats. There's definitely some violent imagery. But it's still pretty ambiguous. Private security might be something to look into. I can give you some names. Like you said, it might just be an obsessed fan. Or someone who's obsessed with what happened to you and your friends. We run across some of these 'murder groupies' from time to time. And your case was so high profile, and you're so well known now, that it's not surprising that someone might be fixated on you. Hell, I studied you in college."

"My books?"

"No, no. Well, I read a few of those. Like I said, my wife is a fan, and I was trying to impress her. They're good, just not really my cup of tea. But, what I meant was that your case was in our criminology textbooks. Unfortunately, it's a matter of academic record."

"Oh Christ," she said.

"I know it's painful being forced to relive these things."

She shook her head. "No, it isn't. It's not 'painful.' You know what it is? It's fucking boring. It's tiresome. It's a horrific thing that happened to me, but it's a fact of life. It's just there. But to these people it's something lurid and exciting. It's so predictable to be obsessed with something like this. Some pathetic, angry little nothing of a person, who feels like a badass by imitating another pathetic angry nothing who butchered young girls. And of course that's what it's really about. Killing young women. And then these people who don't sympathize with a murderer, but they still want to live vicariously through me. They want a piece of what happened to me and they want to feel better about their lives by comparing it to mine. I just want to scream at them, you weren't there when I watched my best friends die and you weren't there when I laid in the hospital for two weeks and you weren't there when I had to shit in a bag for months, because they had to take out part of my intestines. So, you don't get to live vicariously through me."

"You know," he said. "I know some criminology professors who would love to have you speak in their classes. I'm not even kidding. Those students could learn a lot from you."

"No thanks," she said. "But I'm writing a book about it now. If I ever finish it, maybe it can be required reading. At least someone will read it."

"Well, I'll definitely read a copy. I'm sure your insight will be far more informative than what I've read about the case so far."

"Detective," she said. "I appreciate you stopping by, but if there's nothing else, I feel gross, and I'd really like to take a shower and then get to work."

"No," he said. "I've kept you long enough. I wish there was more we could do to help. I'll give you my card. It has my cell number. If you need anything, give me a call."

She got up to take the card, but her leg was still stiff and she grimaced and limped for a moment.

"You've got some battle scars, huh?"

She smiled a thin smile.

"I've got a few of those," he said. "I was in Afghanistan." He looked over at Anthony. "You too, I bet."

Cassandra liked the way he said it. Conversational. Often people tried to tell her about their injuries as though they were proud and they thought that it gave them some connection to her. Like they were members of some exclusive club and they had just showed her the secret handshake. Conley was just mentioning it.

"We'll be in touch. I'll let Mr. Lucas know if anything relevant comes up." He started towards the door, and Anthony went to show him out.

"Wait," said Cassandra. "Just a minute." She went to a box on the table next to her writing desk and got out a copy of her latest book. She got a pen off of the desk. "What's your wife's name?"

"Megan."

"With an 'H'?"

"Without."

She inscribed the book, "To Megan, Blessed Be" and signed her name and gave it to Conley.

"Thank you so much for doing that," he beamed. "She'll be thrilled."

After Conley left, Anthony gathered up the coffee cups and said he would make breakfast while she showered.

"Fine," she said. "But, then you have to go. I need to work."

"I will. I'm going to go back to Portland for a bit. But, I'm coming back here tonight and spending the night. Again, this is not optional. Sutton House is dragging their feet over whether or not they'll help pay for security for you and until that's straightened out, we're roommates."

"Whatever," she sighed. "But, you have to sit in your car until I'm done working."

"Okay," he said. "Ya know, I think the Detective might have been flirting with you a little bit. And if I didn't know any better, I'd say you were letting him."

She shut the bathroom door in his face and turned on the shower. When she was done showering, Anthony was gone. He had left a pan of scrambled eggs with bits of ham on the stove. She ate them quickly right from the pan while brewing more coffee. The pan in the sink and a cup of fresh strong coffee on her desk, she sat down to work. She cued up the playlist that she had put together for this next section.

When interviewers asked, as they often did, what she required to be able to work, she invariably answered "music and coffee." Music was part of the ritual. She chose music based on what mood she wanted to evoke with her writing. Putting together a playlist was a part of plotting out the story; as she thought about where the story would go next, she would also find the songs that conjure the necessary mood. She played some of her old records as she was writing, if the mood called for it. If she needed to time travel back to 1990. But, most of the time, a playlist on her computer was enough.

She wrote for hours, in focused concentration. She took one

142

break, after two hours, when her bladder refused to be ignored any longer. Stretched and made more coffee. And then another sprint of almost two hours. The words flowed out of her, the way writers think they're supposed to, but they seldom do. That rare groove where the brain and the fingers are in perfect rhythm and you just type without thinking. When it's good like that, writing really is like sprinting. More often though, it's closer to mountain climbing. Slow and deliberate.

The hours passed and her back grew stiff and her fingers numb and her bladder once again nagged her about all of that coffee she was drinking. Three thousand words and she felt satisfied that she could call it a night. It was getting dark out and a light rain was starting to fall. She saved her file and opened her browser to check email.

Cassandra had a rule when she was working not to go online or check email until after she had written. It was too easy to procrastinate until the desire to work was gone. In her early years she had struggled, as many writers do, with self-motivation. But like all successful writers she had taught herself discipline, had learned to prioritize her work above other things. In addition, she had also found that going online before she wrote had a negative effect on her work. It ruined her mood, and the sordidness of the outside world insinuated itself into her writing. So she set rules for herself.

She opened her email and scanned the hundreds of unread messages in her inbox. In the early days of email, Anthony had helped her sort through it. But eventually he had come to the decision that corralling her inbox was not a job for a manager, or executive assistant, or whatever his title was. He nagged her for years to hire a personal assistant, but she refused to let another person into her life. Anthony told her about virtual assistants. You'll never even have to meet them, they do every-thing online! But she still didn't like the idea of trusting a new person to look through her email. So, she simply allowed the flood of unread messages to continue. And any time Anthony asked about it, she would insist that she had it under control. Most of what came in could be ignored, anyway. If it was something important, like an editor or her accountant, she usually noticed it. Or if she missed it, they would contact Anthony after a few days and he would call her. So, in a way, he was still screening her emails for her. It just wasn't voluntary anymore.

A message near the top caught her eye. The subject line was just a number. Nine digits. The number looked familiar, and it took her a moment to realize that it was her Social Security number. She picked up her phone and called Anthony. He answered right away, which meant that he was driving and had his headset on.

"What's wrong?" he asked.

"Nothing. I don't know. Why do you think something's wrong?"

"Do you know how long it's been since you called me, instead of me calling you?"

"No. I don't."

He waited a moment for her to speak. When she didn't he asked again, "So, why are you calling me?"

"Well," she said. "A curious thing. Someone sent me an email with my Social Security number as the subject line."

"Okay. Probably some kind of scam. Trying to get your personal info so they can steal your identity."

"I thought your Social Security number was what they try to steal. If they already have that, what else do they need? And why email me to tell me they have it?"

"Fair enough," he said. "Who is it from?"

"The address is just a bunch of random letters."

"So, what does the email say?"

"I didn't open it. I didn't know if it was a virus or something."

"Your email program scans for viruses. As long as you don't open any attachments, you should be fine. Besides, if it was a virus, the subject would be something that would make you want to open it, not something that makes you suspicious. It's usually something about Asian mail-order brides or penis enlargement."

"Yeah, I don't get those. I think that's just you."

"Well, they don't know me very well, then. Or they would know that I'm not interested in brides. And I definitely don't need…"

She cut him off. "Okay, that's fine. You can stop right there."

"Just open the email and see what it says."

She opened the email and saw what it said:

*Cassandra-*

*U DONT KNOW ME BUT U WILL. I AM THE HEIR TO THE LEGACY OF THE HUNTSMAN. I CARRY ON HIS WORK. CHARLOTTE KNOWS ME AND SO DOES MARIAN. THEY HAVE SEEN MY WORK FIRSTHAND. THEY R WITH ELISE AND THE OTHERS. IN HELL.*

*I AM THE POACHER.*

"WELL," said Anthony. "What does it say?"

"I don't want to read this to you."

"Why? What's the matter? Look, just forward it to me and I'll pull over and read it. Hang on, I'll put you on hold while I open my email."

She clicked the forward button, and he pulled over to the shoulder. She waited a few minutes, and he came back on the line.

"I'm on my way back. I'll be there in an hour."

"Okay," she said. "Anthony, do I have to ask who Charlotte and Marian are? Or do I already know?"

"You already know," he said.

# TRACK 10: THE SKY IS A POISONOUS GARDEN

We ran along the road. We didn't see a car. But, I heard one. I heard the engine crank and start up in the driveway behind us. That didn't make sense. We were in a horror movie, running from the monster. The monster isn't supposed to just get into an old beat up Dodge Ram and fire it up and chase you in it. Jason didn't just drive after his victims. I heard the tires crunching the gravel of the driveway as it backed out. And then the headlights swept across us as it turned into the road. I heard the clunk and grind of its old transmission being put into gear.

We had been running for several minutes and we had made it almost a football field away, but it would only take the truck a few seconds to close that distance. He would... I don't know, run us down? Plow into us and send us ragdolling into the ditch so he could take his time with our limp, broken bodies? We had to get off the road. I said, "Come on," but Elise already knew.

We ran off the road and started down the small embankment to a farmer's field. There was a fence about three feet high, but the bank was so steep that we were almost level with the top of it. The truck was only a few yards away now, shifting through the gears and picking up speed. We didn't have time to think, just jumped. We were girls, and we teased our hair and wore makeup and fishnets. But we were still poor kids from the rural South. We knew how to cross fences and jump creeks and climb trees.

Elise cleared the fence and came down hard on the other side, stumbled a little, but got back to her feet. I jumped just a split-second too early, was an inch too short. My toe caught on the top of the fence as I went over, tripping me up and causing me to land face first on the ground.

Pain shot through my shoulder, and the impact knocked the wind out of me. I was laying in a muck of mud, fetid water, and more than a little cow shit. Elise grabbed me by the collar and a handful of hair and yanked me forward and onto my feet. My whole body hurt and I'm sure hers did too. But, we started running again. Because the truck had pulled up even with where we had jumped the fence. I think he must have stopped for a moment to think about whether he should jump the fence too. Probably thought about the head start we had. And the risk of leaving the truck there and maybe drawing attention.

I heard him rev the engine and pop the clutch and take off, flinging gravel and mud behind him. He drove off along the fence, looking for a gate so he could run us down in the open field. Did we scream for help? Of course, as much as possible while running as fast as we could. Try it some time. Running full speed, you can barely talk, let alone scream. There wasn't a house within a mile of us, anyway.

"I have to stop!" I said.

"We can't stop," Elise said.

"I *have* to! I can't breathe!" I was going to hyperventilate. I went down on my hands and knees and tried to slow my breathing. It was coming in gasps, and I thought I would pass out. I choked and coughed and hacked up some phlegm and some of the disgusting muck that I hadn't even realized I had inhaled. Elise was rubbing my back, saying over and over, "Come on, Cass. Come on. We gotta go." I stood up, breathing heavy. I was light-headed, and I stumbled a little.

I looked around. We were in the middle of a field. It was dark and quiet, and I could hear cows shuffling around in the dark. I could see stars and the lights of town off in the distance. What were we afraid of? I had thought we were running from someone, but that's crazy. Things like that don't happen. We were just out in the middle of a field. There are cows here. I remember thinking that meant everything was okay, because bad things don't happen in places where cows live. Elise was shouting at me for some reason.

"Come on! We have to go!"

We started running again. We ran across the field and we could see lights up ahead getting closer. The ground was uneven, and we stumbled a few times, but never fell. Suddenly the ground leveled out. We had come to a muddy road, cutting through the field. That made my stomach sink, but I couldn't figure out why. Then I realized why, when I heard a truck engine in the distance, over the hill.

Maybe there was a gate and he wouldn't get through. That hope died when I heard the engine rev and a metallic clang and crash. Of course, he would just drive through the gate. We saw headlights shine through the dark trees at the edge of the field. They were less than half a mile away. They would sweep across the road in a few minutes and he would see us. We ran across the road and through the field, hoping we could get over the crest of the next hill and he wouldn't see us. I could see his headlights now, two round glowing eyes at the edge of the field. The truck bounced along the rutted muddy road. I saw another light. He had a spotlight, and he was sweeping it back and forth on either side of the truck, searching the fields for us.

Keep running. Keep running.

Keep running. We were over the rise a little, but would it be enough, or would he still be able to see us? Elise was a little ahead of me. She stopped suddenly, almost tripping over something in the dark. It was a low cement wall, less than two feet high. The foundation of some building, a shed or a barn or maybe even a house. Everything else was long gone, but the cement footer would stand for a hundred more years. "Get down," said… one of us. I don't even remember who. Maybe both of us. We dropped to the ground behind the footer and laid flat.

I was on my stomach and there was a sharp rock digging into my hip and some unidentified wetness seeping through my skirt at the knee. I remember wishing that I had laid face up so I could look at the stars. Maybe then I could pretend we were just out laying in my backyard, stargazing. I didn't dare turn over, though. I inched my hand underneath me enough to push the rock out from under my hip. Elise hissed at me, "be still." It was little more than a breath. We were face to face, and it was so quiet we could hear each other breathing and our breaths seemed impossibly loud.

The truck's engine was a low rumble, getting steadily closer. And the popping of gravel under the tires. Getting louder. God, why is he going so slow? I thought. At this rate, it will take him an hour to pass by us. I lifted my head up enough to see the spotlight sweep across the field a few feet away from us, and then it was gone. He must have been aiming it at the other side now. A crazy panicked urge told me to get up and run, go now while he's looking the other way. I clenched my fists and put the thought out of my mind. It would only be a minute until he swept it back our way and then he would see us.

Suddenly everything around us was bright as day. He was shining the spotlight right at us. Or right at the footer. I pushed my face into the dirt. I tried to be as still and small as possible. I thought of playing hide and seek when I was little. Thinking that if I concentrated hard enough on being invisible, no one would find me, even though my feet were sticking out from under the curtain. The light seemed to stay on us far longer than it had on the spots I had seen before. Did you know we were there? Did he suspect? Did he see the footer and think it was a likely hiding place? Finally the light went away and I let my breath out. The truck kept moving. We relaxed a little. Just wait until he's down the road and then get up and run again.

I heard a metallic, grinding squeal. He was putting on the brakes. He was stopping. Then the gears grinding and the truck was moving again, but it sounded different now and you don't really ever pay attention to the fact that cars sound different when they're in reverse. But, I noticed it now, and I knew that he was backing up. Did he see something? Did we give ourselves away somehow? And then it hit me. Oh god, our footprints. The road was muddy. He must have seen our footprints in the mud. He backed up and stopped, and the light was on us again. We looked at each other, craning our necks to see without lifting our heads. She was scared, too. What do we do? If he knows we're here, we should run. Get as much of a head start as possible. But if he's not sure, we should stay put and not give ourselves away. The light didn't move. Then the light went out.

Then the engine revved louder than it had before and there was a noise of tires spinning and clawing in dirt and mud and a dimmer light swept across and we looked at each other and realized at the same time what he was doing. He was driving across the field, straight for us. Without a word, we both jumped to our feet and suddenly there in the headlights, we could see each other for the first time since the house and we were covered in blood and mud and we looked like refugees from Hell.

We ran. He would have to drive around the footer, which would give us a few seconds. But it wouldn't be enough, would it? We ran as hard as we could. My legs burned. My lungs burned. We went at a diagonal to try to stay out of his headlights, but he just turned with us. In hindsight, I guess we should have split up. He could only chase one of us. Splitting up would have given one of us a chance. But we never even thought of that. For me, at least, the thought of being alone, of being separated from her, was unthinkable. I know some people reading this will judge me, will think Elise might have survived if I had been strong enough to take my chances alone. Maybe he would have followed me and she would have gotten away. Think that if you want. Because I've thought it myself a thousand times.

He closed on us, but not as fast as you might think. He had to continually change course. Rocks that we ran around would have torn the engine out of the truck. Shrubs that we passed through easily would have hung him up. Still, he got closer. And then we ran straight off a cliff.

That's how it felt, anyway. The ground dropped out from underneath us and we slid down a slope of wet sticky red clay into waist-high water so cold it took our breath away. My left leg bent underneath me and my knee collided with a rock at the bottom. It felt like something snapped in there, but it was just another pain to add to the list. When we stood up, we were in an irrigation ditch about five feet deep. I could just see over the top of it. We scrambled up the other side, clawing in the wet clay. Dragging, pushing each other until we were across. The truck skidded to a stop on the other side. If he had driven just another foot, he would have gone nose-first into the ditch. That would have been a hell of a thing to try to explain the next morning, wouldn't it?

We started running again. There was no way the truck could get across. It just sat there with the engine idling, like he was trying to decide what to do. Should he cross the ditch and chase us on foot? Drive around and try to cut us off up ahead? Either way, we were getting farther and farther away from him. We ran at an angle again to get out of his headlights.

I thought for sure my heart was going to burst. My lungs felt like they were on fire. My legs were turning to liquid and would give out at any moment. But we kept running because the woods at the edge of the field loomed ahead of us and if we could get to the trees, we could hide. I heard the truck door slam behind us and then the spotlight started to sweep wildly around, looking for us. We were only a few feet away from the treeline now. I was slightly ahead of Elise now. She was faster, but I guess my endurance was a little better and she was slowing down a bit. We made it to the treeline, and I felt a surge of relief. And then I realized, just a second too late, that there was a barbed wire fence strung between the trees. There was no time to stop my momentum, and I ran right into it. The force of the impact made the wires stretch and sag a little, but they held. I folded over at the waist, draped across the fence, and my weight caused the barbs to dig into me.

"Oh my God!" said Elise. She must have thought I was dead. But then I exhaled a groan of pain. Some instinct in me must have compelled me to continue my forward movement, because I pushed off with my feet and let my torso drop the rest of the way over the fence. As I tumbled across, the barbs sliced long furrows through my flesh and then I landed with a thud on the other side. Searing pain made my eyes water, and I thought to myself that I should just lay there. Just wait for whatever was going to happen. Elise was scrambling across the fence now. It was easier for her, since I had been nice enough to tear out a few of the staples that held the wires in place. She grabbed my hand and pulled me up. She didn't even check to see if I was still alive. I think that if I was dead, she would have just dragged me behind her.

"Come on!" she said, when I started to show signs of life. "We made it! We have a chance to get away now!"

She was right. We were in the trees. We would have places to hide. The forest was always our sanctuary. Our place to hide. We can just live here, I thought. We'll stay here and he'll never find us. We'll make a little home and we'll heal and grow stronger. And then someday, we'll come back to take our vengeance. Elise pulled me forward, but slower now. We could catch our breath and regain a little of our strength. We stumbled through the trees and the laurel thickets. If it was Summer, the woods would have been too thick with honeysuckle and blackberries to walk through. Since it was Fall, our steps crunched over a carpet of dead leaves, but we didn't try to be quiet. There wasn't time for that.

We were streaked with blood and mud and cow shit. Soaked to the waist from the irrigation ditch. The cuts on my sides from the window glass and the barbed wire burned and stung with every step, and I knew that there was blood trickling down my hips and mixing with the water. I can't imagine what Elise's hand must have felt like. We made short dashes and stopped to hide behind trees. Look behind us to see if he was following. It was too dark to see anything. We tried to listen for movement, but all I could hear was my own ragged breaths and my heart thumping in my ears. There wasn't much point in hiding "behind" trees, because he could have just as easily come up on us from the other direction. We dashed again and then stopped and heard running water. A little creek, no more than a foot across. We knelt and used the water to wash our faces and drank a little. It was achingly cold. We heard something move.

We froze in place. We were already crouched down and there was a big tree next to us. So, we crawled as close to its trunk as we could, crouched down small. I tried to quiet my breathing and looked around at the darkness. Just vague shapes. Nothing moving. But then we heard it again. Something big, moving, not far from us. It moved slow, brushing against branches, footfalls breaking sticks. Coming closer now. The bushes rustled twenty feet away. Stand still. Don't move. It's dark and maybe he won't see us and maybe he'll pass by. A shape emerged from the bushes and we could see the dark silhouette.

A deer. She walked to the creek and dipped her muzzle in and drank. We breathed a sigh of relief and she jerked her head up and looked our way. Frozen for a heartbeat and then she took off back the way she had come.

We went around the tree to make another dash. The Huntsman was on the other side of the tree, waiting for us.

# 11

She called the number on the card Detective Conley had given her. It rang several times before she thought to look at the clock. It was almost ten. She tried to remember what time "normal people" went to bed and was thinking about hanging up when a woman answered.

Suddenly being confronted with a new person whom she had never spoken to made her stammer nervously. "I'm sorry. I was trying to reach Detective Conley. I might have dialed wrong."

"No, you have the right number. This is his wife."

Cassandra couldn't help but notice the emphasis she put on the word "wife."

"I'm… he's helping me with a case. I'm sorry to bother you so late, but… something happened. And I'd like to talk to him. If it's not too late. I'm sorry, I hate talking on the phone and I'm not very good at it."

"No, no worries. You're doing fine. I hate the phone, too. Hold on just a sec, he's getting out of the shower."

"I can call back later. Or he can call me…"

"No, it's fine. It'll be just a minute."

There was an awkward silence for a moment, and

Cassandra wondered if she was supposed to be saying something. Before she could think better of it, she blurted out, "So, you're Megan?"

"Um, maybe. How do you know my name?"

Her face burned red "I was just wondering if you got the book?" Another thing she shouldn't have said. Maybe he was saving it to give to her on her birthday or something. Cassandra decided she needed to just stop talking entirely. Maybe hang up.

"I did!" Megan said. "Is this Cassandra?"

"Yes."

"Thank you so much for the book. You have no idea what it means to me. He mentioned that he met you. He wasn't supposed to do that, I hope you don't mind."

"No, it's fine. I gave him permission to tell you. He told me about your shop. It's sounds lovely."

"Well, it's mostly a lot of touristy stuff. I do have some nice crystals and a few interesting books."

"I'll have to stop in some time."

"I don't know what's taking him so long."

"You know," Cassandra said. "Maybe you can be of help to me."

"Me?"

"Yes. Did your husband tell you anything about my case?"

"Oh no. He never discusses the specifics of his cases with me."

"Well, I'm trying to find a spell. I have plenty of warding spells to keep people away. But I can't find a spell to attract someone to me. I only have a few books and to be honest they're pretty basic."

"None of them have love spells?"

"No, I'm not looking for a love spell. I'm looking for a spell to attract someone to me who isn't a lover. In fact, it's someone I despise."

"Well, I can't think of any spells like that."

"That's okay. I figured it couldn't hurt to ask."

"You could always write a spell yourself."

"I've actually never written any of my own spells."

"What?! But, you're a writer."

Cassandra sighed. "I know. It's embarrassing, but for some reason I just can't do it. My brain doesn't think that way. It only thinks in stories."

"Well, I can look through my books and see if I can find something."

"No, I don't want you to go to any trouble."

"It's okay. I'm kind of intrigued now. If I find anything I'll… is it okay to text you back at this number?"

"Of course. But really you don't have to…. "

"It's no trouble. Besides it's not every day that one of your favorite authors asks you for a favor."

"Thank you, I'm flattered. Oh, and could you not mention this to your husband?"

"Don't worry, I don't talk about that kind of stuff with him. He doesn't listen, anyway. Oh, speak of the devil!"

Cassandra heard the phone changing hands, and then Conley came on the line. "Hello?"

"It's Cassandra Watson."

"Hi. So what were you and Megan chatting about?"

"Oh, you know, girl stuff. Makeup, hair, The Backstreet Boys."

"Okay, okay. So what's up?"

She told him about the emails. He knew the names and what they signified right away.

"Well," he said. "This is good, in a way. This is a clear, tangible threat. And him mentioning the other girls' names will make it easier to link him to those murders when we catch him."

"If you catch him."

"No, when. It may not be OSP that gets him, but someone will. He's got the California Highway Patrol and the FBI looking for him. One of us will get this guy."

"Hopefully I'll be alive to see it."

"Don't talk that way. You'll be fine. Are you there by yourself?"

"I am, but Anthony is on his way back."

"Okay, that's good. Do you have an alarm system?"

"No, I used to for the first year I lived here, but the squirrels kept setting it off, so I got rid of it. I didn't think I would ever need it."

"Okay, just keep your doors locked, and the blinds closed. If you hear anything unusual, call 911 and then call me. I don't think this guy would break in, though. He's not that brave. He's more the lie-in-wait type."

"I hope you're right."

"Forward me the email. I'll see if it's possible to track it. It's unlikely though, emails are just way too easy to anonymize. But we might come up with something."

He gave her his email address and assured her again that everything would be fine. They hung up, and she forwarded the email to him. Later that night, she got a text from Megan.

ANTHONY WALKED UP onto her porch. He stopped at the door. There was a symbol drawn there in white. A five-pointed star. Then he noticed other symbols on the floor. He knew a little about witchcraft. Being Cassandra's manager for almost twenty years, he had picked up a few things. Although he didn't know exactly what they meant, he knew a sigil when he saw one. He opened the front door and called out, "Cass?"

"I'm here," she said. "Watch your step." He looked down as he entered and saw a line of something white. He stepped over it.

"What is that?" he asked.

"Salt."

"Did you seriously leave the front door unlocked? Are you nuts?" He stepped inside. The room was dark, lit only by the candles burning on the coffee table. She was sitting on the couch, staring into the flames, and she seemed to be deep in concentration. The room had a dry, dusty smell of burning leaves.

"No," said Cassandra. "I'm not nuts. I'm just not afraid anymore. I've determined to let go of my fear and my negative energy. And I've taken steps to protect myself."

"What steps?" he asked. "Drawing sigils? A salt circle? Burning…" he sniffed the air. "Is that sage?"

"Yes," she said. "And other herbs. I burned them to purify my space and rid it of the negative energy that this man has inflicted on me. And yes, I drew protective sigils on the porch and made a circle of salt around the outside wall. I have also recited some words of protection. I know you don't believe in these things, but please try not to let your skepticism taint the atmosphere."

"You know I respect your beliefs. And with all due respect, sigils and salt circles may not be enough to keep this guy away."

She laughed a little. He couldn't remember the last time he had seen her laugh. In fact, he couldn't remember the last time he had seen her so calm. Definitely not since she had finished her last book. She was always calm when she was in the midst of writing, when the words were flowing well. The anxieties came back when it became time to release the book into the world. And when she started a new book, still trying to fit the story's puzzle pieces together.

"I can't believe you're this calm just from cleansing the energy of your house."

"Well, I also started taking my anti-anxiety meds again. So that probably helps."

"At any rate, keeping the door locked is just common sense."

"A locked door won't keep him out," she said. "It wouldn't even slow him down. No, I'll just wait for him to come. He's going to do what he's going to do. And I'm going to do what I'm going to do."

"And what's that?" He came in and sat on a chair next to the couch.

"I'm still planning," she said. "But, I've dealt with his type before. He doesn't know what he's getting himself into."

"Okay," he said. "You've dealt with someone like this before. But it left you, well... damaged. Sorry, I can't think of a better word. I don't want you to have to go through something like that again."

"I appreciate that. But, I've learned a lot since then. I'm stronger now. I was a little girl then. Since I got that email, I've been thinking, about what happened before, and about this man who is killing these girls and sending me these messages. Men like that, they feed off of fear, it's what gives them their power. If you stop fearing them, you take away their power. You never truly understood witchcraft, and that's fine. You understand me, so you don't need to understand it. And I never really made an effort to explain it to you.

"The main thing you have to understand about it, is that it's not about making things happen. It's about knowing they will happen and letting them. It's not about gaining power, it's about allowing power to flow through you. And the power is always there, trying to flow through you. If there is a pile of sticks blocking a stream and you remove those sticks, that doesn't mean that you caused the water to flow. You removed an obstruction that was keeping the water from doing what is in its nature. Does that make sense?"

"I guess," he said. "But, you're the writer. The artist. You know I'm more literal-minded. You're the intellectual and I'm more about action. I'm not really seeing how this is a plan of action for dealing with this situation."

"But, you see, that's the point. This is all about action. Witchcraft is all about taking action to effect change in your life. About using the forces at your disposal to change things. I know the way I described it, saying that it's about letting things happen, makes it sound passive. But, it's not. Your will has to be in harmony with the nature of the forces that you're using. You remove the obstruction so the water can flow, but you can't make it flow uphill. It's still going to do what's in its nature to do. And while you can't take credit for the water flowing, it was your action that allowed it to flow. I realized this, or remembered it. Life is about taking action. Making things happen, instead of waiting for things to happen to you. I'm not going to sit here passively and wait for this guy to come and try to kill me. Or whatever the hell he has in mind."

"Well," he said. "Hopefully it won't come to that. But, I'll sleep on the couch tonight. And I'll call Detective Conley in the morning."

"I already called him and briefed him on the situation. And I forwarded the email to him."

"Okay. I guess there's nothing for me to do but sleep over then."

"You don't have to sleep on the couch. I cleared off the bed in the spare room for you."

"There was a bed under all those boxes? Well, thank you, I appreciate it. Are you writing anymore tonight?"

"No, I got it out of my system for the night. I'll be sleeping late tomorrow. I have a lot of thinking and planning to do tonight. So, don't invite any of your cop buddies over too early, okay?"

More emails came in that night. She knew they would. She

didn't even mention them to Anthony, who sat on the bed in the spare room conducting business on his phone. She could have almost guessed what they would say.

Each one was a single line:

YOU'RE SO CLOSE.

FINAL SOLUTION.

AND FINALLY, inevitably: *Cuts You Up.*

WAS HE CLOSE BY? Sending messages from his phone? Or hunched over a laptop in a motel room? Maybe he was somewhere on the other side of the country, trying to scare her from afar. No, she knew that wasn't true. He was coming, would be there soon. She could feel him approaching, like a storm on the horizon. He'll come, she thought. And I'll be ready this time.

# TRACK 11: I AM MISERY

The Huntsman was on the other side of the tree, waiting for us. He stood motionless as a part of the forest. Hooded and faceless. He might have been a rock or a stump, and I had a strange notion that he had been there the whole time we stumbled through the woods. Waiting for us to find him. We stopped short, shifted our weight against our momentum, tried to pivot. But it was too quick. We were too close. Elise was too close. I saw his hand move. I thought he was drawing back to slap her, but the hand he swung held the knife and he chopped, hacked, slashed... I don't know what the right word is and I don't give a shit.

The knife collided with her torso, right under the armpit, right at her ribcage and he drew it across. She shrieked. I had never heard her scream like that, even when she broke her ankle in gym class. I had never heard anyone scream like that. She collapsed to the ground and curled up into herself and lay still. Then it was my turn.

I turned and tried to run, but he was on me so fast and then I was facedown on the ground and he was on my back, straddling me and yanking a handful of hair and I thought he would just pull my head back and slit my throat. And maybe he thought about that. Just dispose of us and be done with it. But then his true nature took over. It was no fun if it was quick. It was unsatisfying. He needed to take his time and enjoy the pain he was inflicting.

He yanked my hair and grabbed my arm to turn me over, and then I was on my back and he was on top of me again. He had me pinned again before I could move, arms jammed down by my sides, his knees on top of them. Sitting on my stomach. His whole weight right there on my sternum, so I could barely breathe. He slowly lowered the blade to my face, let me feel the cold metal. Wet with blood. Wet with Elise's blood. And Joey's. He must have been smearing the blood on my cheek. Reveling in my fear and revulsion. Then he slid it back the other way, like he was shaving my cheek, letting me feel the sharp edge grabbing at my skin, but not quite letting it cut into me.

He was muttering something to himself, but I couldn't understand it. He was close enough that I could smell his breath and it smelled like cigarettes and tooth decay. To this day I'll occasionally catch a whiff of someone's breath and it will smell like that and I'll be overcome with nausea. He was that close, and I still couldn't understand what he was saying to himself. Like it wasn't even real words.

He jammed his left hand down on my throat. To hold me in place. So I couldn't move. So I couldn't breathe or scream. He pushed my head back, and I was looking away from him, but my vision was starting to blur, anyway. I waited to feel the blade on my neck. But I didn't. I felt it on my chest. He wanted my heart. The blade sliced through my shirt, and then I felt the strap of my bra sever. I felt the edge of the blade dig into my skin and then white hot pain and I bucked and tried to move, but he was leaning with all of his weight on my neck.

It was so slow. I felt the blade cut deeper and deeper and every second was pain like I had never felt before. And then the next second was worse. I screamed. Somehow I screamed, even though he was pressing down on my windpipe. Maybe I was only screaming in my head. It went on and on. He drew out the agony. Slicing through my breast. Taking his time destroying it. Focusing his rage on that part of the anatomy that symbolized sex, motherhood, femininity. The things he hated most. Or maybe it was just an obstacle to cut through to get to the heart. His ultimate goal.

I pissed myself. I didn't know or care at the time. But if I'm laying this bare, then there it is. That's how we die, in such misery and fear that we lose control of our bodily functions and don't even notice. In the end, we're just masses of flesh and bodily fluids. And there was no doubt in my mind that this was the end.

Except somehow it wasn't. I don't know if I blacked out or if the memories are just blurred. I just know that suddenly he stopped cutting, and he released the pressure on my throat and I gasped and drew in air and my head cleared and that was worse. Because the pain was suddenly immediate and undeniable. My whole world was pain.

He had made a mistake. He was so eager to inflict pain on me that he forgot about Elise. Or he thought she was dead. He could have killed me quickly and then returned to make sure she was dead. But he didn't. And she regained her strength and sat up and forced her mind to focus through her agony and see him straddling me, cutting into me. I don't know what she did, but when my head cleared, he was on his back and she was kicking him in the face. She saved my life.

We made a mistake too. We let him live. We had him on the ground. The knife was laying next to him. We should have finished him off. Butchered him like a pig. Like he had butchered all the others. Like he had tried to butcher us and would try to again. But we didn't. We hadn't given up our humanity yet. Didn't know that it was already gone and that no matter what we did, we would never be whole again. We still thought that if we made it through this, we could go back to normal. So we ran.

I don't remember how long we ran through the woods, holding ourselves, trying to keep the blood in. Trying to keep ourselves from falling apart. I had thought that Elise was dead, but here she was, running right with me. So she must be fine, I thought. She ran sort of hunched over, holding her stomach, but she seemed okay. We must have left a trail of blood behind us, must have painted the woods red. When I pictured it in my mind later, I imagined we were like the playing cards in "Alice In Wonderland" slopping red paint on the rose bushes. I held my coat tight to my chest, feeling the blood seep through. Trying not to think about what my chest must look like underneath, the razor incision disfiguring me.

I don't know how we had the strength to run. It must have been pure adrenalin, pure fight-or-flight. Raw animal survival instinct. I was cold, colder than I thought it was possible to be and still be alive. The kind of cold that I imagine the dead feel when they're six feet underground. I was getting light-headed, and my vision started to blur again. Sounds seemed to pulse and echo and it reminded me of when I had gotten laughing gas at the dentist.

We ran for minutes or hours or years and we would crash into bushes or bounce off trees. Stumble over rocks and cut ourselves on thorns. But pain was meaningless now. Another sensation. We swam in an ocean of pain, so what did it matter if a few more raindrops fell on us? We were probably twenty feet beyond the treeline, before we realized that we had run out of the woods. We stopped, wobbling in our tracks and looked around us. We were in an open field and there was a large building surrounded by security lights in front of us. It took a moment to sink in where we were.

We were in the practice football field behind our high

school. We had been here a few hours before, but that seemed like something that had happened to different people. It didn't seem possible that the horror we were going through could happen less than a quarter of a mile from where we learned about calculus and gossiped about classmates and ate fish sticks dipped in ketchup. But there it was, there was the cafeteria. There were the picnic tables we had sat on earlier that afternoon, sneaking a smoke and planning our adventure.

We ran across the field to the school and I don't know what we thought we would do when we got there. Except that maybe when we were bathed in the eerie glow of the security lights and when we touched the solid doors of this familiar building, that we would come back to reality. Because, how could running from a murderer with a huge knife coexist in the same reality with the building where Mr. Snellings droned on about the Articles of Confederation?

We got to the door and yanked on the handle even though we knew it would be locked. It was a formality. And there we were, dripping blood on the cement that still showed the stain from when I had spilled chocolate milk a week before. And it was still real. We didn't wake up from the nightmare. We didn't see him anywhere, but there was no doubt that he would follow.

We had to get inside. There would be places to hide, weapons we could use, a phone to call the police. We yanked ineffectually on the door a few more times. We looked around for some way to get in and then I saw a cinder block sitting against the wall. The cinder block they used to prop the cafeteria door open when the weather was warm, because whatever mechanism was supposed to hold the door open was broken and this was cheaper than getting it fixed. I grabbed the block and was about to swing it at the glass of the doors, but then I noticed that there was wire mesh in the glass to keep it from being broken. I held the block and looked around, then

I raised it above my head and I could feel the wound on my chest pull open as I stretched my arm up and I threw the block as hard as I could at the closest cafeteria window. The glass cracked and splintered, but it held. The cinder block bounced back and landed on the ground. I collapsed to my knees from the effort of throwing the block, and I started to cry.

Elise wasn't sad though, she was pissed off. She always got mad when things didn't go the way they were supposed to, even if the object of her anger was inanimate. If it had been her car that we had been riding in and that left us stranded, she might have thrown a rock through its windshield. She went and grabbed the cinder block and strode up to the window. She drew back the block like a batter waiting for a pitch and swung the block as hard as she could. She grunted in frustration, and the block broke when it hit the glass. But it was enough. The glass shattered inward. She walked over and took me by the hands and guided me to my feet and we took turns climbing through the broken window and then sat on the floor in the broken glass, with our backs to the wall. We weren't safe, but we felt safer. It was warmer inside, at least. The dark outlines of the tables where we ate lunch every day seemed strange, so quiet and empty. For a crazy second I thought that we would get in trouble for bleeding on the cafeteria floor.

"We have to call the police," she said finally. I had hoped that breaking the window would set off an alarm, but there was no sound.

We got up slowly, peering over the ledge of the window. We couldn't see anything except the picnic tables bathed in the security light. It was still and silent. Across the cafeteria and out through the doors to the phones in the hallway. There were two payphones. We looked at each other and begun digging in our pockets for change. We both realized at the same time that we didn't have any. The only other phone in the school was in the Principal's office and that was on the other side of the building, behind another locked door. A few years later, I could have just dialed 911, but our county hadn't finished setting up that system yet. To us 911 was just something that people in movies and TV shows used. It was something for people in big cities, something we had never experienced, like getting pizza delivered to your house.

I picked up the receiver and dialed 0 for the operator. I heard it ring, and it was a wonderful sound. I couldn't wait to hear the operator's voice. For the last hour, it had seemed like there wasn't another person on earth except for Elise and me and the killer. All I wanted right then was to hear confirmation that another human being existed. The phone rang again and then there was another sound from inside the cafeteria. The sound of broken glass falling on the floor. We held our breath.

Maybe it was just a shard of glass in the window that had been holding on and finally let go. The operator picked up and said, "How can I help you?" I was about to speak, but just then there was another noise. This one was unmistakable; the sound of a chair sliding a few inches across the linoleum floor. The operator began to speak again, and I quickly put my finger on the cradle to cut her off. Elise gave me a look that asked what the hell I was doing. I put my finger to my lips. I should have said something to the operator, even if it was just "help." She would have known where I was calling from and sent the police. But I panicked. I put the phone quietly back in the cradle and we moved as quickly and silently down the hall as we could.

It was absurd, of course, trying to be quiet. We were leaving a trail of blood that a blind man could follow. But we didn't want him to know how close he was to us. We walked through the maze of dark hallways, looking behind us. Should we hide in a bathroom? No, that would just be cornering ourselves. Lock ourselves in a janitor's closet? We would have to break into it first. My mind raced through possible weapons:

softball bats in the gym, tools in Shop class. Why was he not behind us? Why was he not catching up? Was he toying with us, watching from somewhere? Not seeing him and not knowing how close he was to us was almost worse than having him right behind us.

We turned the corner into the main hallway that led past the Principal's office and he was there. Just standing there. We froze. His back was towards us, and he didn't even know we were there. He was maybe fifteen feet away, and I saw the hood over his head and the knife loose at his side. I realized what he was looking at, why he didn't pay attention to us.

Along the hallway, between the doors to the Administration offices, was a long glass case. It held the trophies from the few times our sports teams had won championships and the plaques commemorating the times we had gone to the finals. But what held his attention was the memorials. Every time a kid at our school died before graduating they put a memorial in this case. A class picture and a little plaque with their name and the year they would have graduated. Going back to the sixties when the school opened. I'd imagine we had far more of those than a school of our size should have. The kids who died in car wrecks and farming accidents. The ones who were shot during hunting season and the Freshman who had leukemia a few years ago. A girl who hanged herself when the captain of the football team dumped her right before prom.

But those didn't interest him, of course. He was looking at the ones he was responsible for, admiring his handiwork. The string of faces from the last few years that we barely glanced at as we walked to class. Their faces were familiar to him, but he had seen them only in darkness, distorted by fear and pain. He was enjoying seeing them smiling for the first time. Gloating over the happiness he had destroyed.

It hadn't sunk in to me before what he was and what he had done. How much misery this man had put into the world.

How many lives he had ruined. I had said I hated people before and my mom would always scold me. "You shouldn't hate anyone," she would say. And I never understood that. Why should I not hate Jenny Miller when she teased me and called me names? But I finally understood. I understood that what I had felt before wasn't true hate. Because I was feeling it, then and I knew I had never felt anything like it before. It was pure, maybe the purest emotion I've ever felt in my life. I suppose if I had been a mother, the love that I felt for my child would have been more pure. But I'm childless, so nothing has ever come close to the hate that I felt for that man, right then.

Elise pulled on my sleeve and tried to get me to move, but I didn't. I was done running.

# 12

S he didn't sleep late. In fact, she barely slept at all. She was nervous and energized and was wide awake as the sun was coming up. She wrote a note and left it on the dining room table:

*Anthony-*

WOKE *early and had to go out and get some things. Be back later. Keep an eye on Jonas and make sure he doesn't get out.*

*-C.*

SHE SLIPPED QUIETLY OUT the front door and started up the old Subaru that she drove maybe once a month. Backed down the driveway and eased down the quiet street. A few of her neighbors were out gardening or hosing the pine needles off of their front walks. They waved at her as she went by. That nice writer lady who lives at the end of the street.

She drove down her street and turned onto the highway. A few miles down, she turned on a small road that led up into the mountains. The forest closed in, thick and dark around her. The land sloped up quickly. Foulweather Bay was a narrow strip of mostly flat land that the ocean had carved into the mountainside over the course of millennia. The incessant damp ocean air made the trees grow fast, and they towered over the narrow, winding road.

She pulled over to the side of the road at the place where she knew that she would lose her cell signal. She made a call to Detective Conley and left him a voicemail. She drove on.

The houses out here weren't as valuable as the ones in town, where you could see the ocean. There were a few expensive log homes, but mostly older houses where loggers and fisherman lived. Little hobby farms. A small park of mobile homes scattered amongst trees. This was where the Ledesmas lived. She had only been there once, when Martha's car had broken down and Cassandra had given her a ride home. The next day she had woken to discover that Jose had walked the five miles to her house to get the car running and drive it home.

She drove on past the mobile homes and then, after a few miles, she turned on a gravel Forest Service road that zigzagged up the side of the mountain. The road was rough and rutted and it ran parallel to a twisting creek. Douglas Firs, Hemlocks, and Sitka Spruce towered above the road. The ground was thick with huge ferns, some several feet across. The woods here were so different from the ones she had played in growing up in Virginia. There the vegetation was much thinner, and you were never more than a mile from a road or a farm. Here, there were miles and miles of nearly impenetrable brush. People can and do get lost in these woods. They were like the primordial forest of fairy tales compared to what she was used to and she was still awed by them, even after having lived amongst them for over a decade.

She hadn't been out here in almost a year, but she remembered the spot when she saw it. This was a place where she came from time to time, when she needed to feel centered. Someone like Anthony might dismiss it as "communing with nature" but, in a way, that's what it was. She came here to remind herself that the world was bigger than herself and that nature is eternal and her problems were insignificant. She felt at home and at peace here, away from the things of the human world.

She pulled over and parked under a massive fir tree, its trunk almost as big as the car. A path led down from the road to a spot by the creek. The trail was damp earth and pine needles, but when she got down to the creek, there was a thick carpet of moss. A small waterfall cascaded and filled the air with mist and music. She carried a blanket down with her and spread it out on the ground and sat down.

She set a small plate that she had brought with her on the ground and piled it high with herbs. Set fire to them with the old Zippo that she had owned since college. She sat and listened to the water and smelled the fragrant smoke, and she began to meditate. She opened her mind to let the forest speak to her. Tell her what she needed to know and what would happen next. She opened her eyes after almost an hour, and she felt calm and refreshed.

This is where I belong, she thought. I haven't been out here in so long, but it's right outside my door. The forest gave me a message that I've strayed too far from my home. This is the same forest I played in as a child. Because there is only one forest and though humans may try to carve it into pieces and divide it with their cities, it is still all one. The rules of nature, of the forest, don't change. They are the same here as they are in Siberia or in India. They are the same now as they were ten thousand years ago. Humanity makes its own rules and divisions, but they are an illusion. They fade and crumble, but the laws of the forest remain.

When she fell into sync with the rhythms of the forest, she felt that she was no different from the sorceress or the shaman or the conjure woman who had lived in the forests of the world since the beginning of time. It was only when she went back to civilization and put her costume back on that she felt disconnected. Lost. Adrift.

I should move out here. Give up the house and find a warm cave to live in. Or build me a little house that can sprout chicken legs and flee whenever someone finds me.

She watched the forest go about its life around her. Chipmunks and birds skittered through the trees. An elk cow moved through the woods across the creek. Looked her way for a moment and then moved along. It felt like a blessing.

The wind had picked up, bringing with it the damp, salty smell of the ocean. Misty fog started to gather in the low spots carved out by the creek. The light became softer. Rain would come soon.

She sat and let her eyes go unfocused. Listened to the forest and what it had to tell her. It told her many things, some that were new to her, some she had once known but had forgotten.

The air changed subtly. The wind whispered to her that something was about to happen. She breathed deep and nodded slowly. I know. I'm ready.

A twig snapped on the path behind her and she turned to look. There was a man standing a few feet away at the edge of the clearing, looking at her. He was in his twenties, pale with thinning hair. He wore a very old, very faded beige canvas jacket and olive drab pants, and he was holding a very long knife. Cassandra stood up very slowly and turned to face him.

"Well," she said. "I guess you're The Poacher?"

He smiled.

She smiled back.

# TRACK 12: DEATHWISH

The Poacher stood a few feet away from me at the edge of the clearing. My smile seemed to confuse him. He seemed unsure of what to do. Likely, this was the first time one of his victims actually looked him in the eye. He jiggled the knife in his hand, eager to use it. It was a butcher knife, the old-fashioned kind. Patinaed blade and carved wooden handle. It was like the one my grandfather had used to butcher hogs and skin bucks. The Poacher took a step toward me and raised the knife. He hesitated again.

"Why aren't you scared?" he asked. His face had the smooth white pallor of bread dough and wore an expression of frustration. He looked like a kid whose favorite toy stopped working.

"Why would I be afraid of you?" I asked.

"Because I am The Poacher," he said. I could hear the note of exasperation he was trying to keep out of his voice. "I carry on the work of The Huntsman. I'm here to finish what he started."

I shook my head. "No. What he started is already finished. I finished it."

"I am The Poacher. I am a hunter. I was born of blood and darkness. I stalk…"

"No. You're a coward who sneaks up on little girls in the dark and kills them before they have a chance to fight back."

He took a few steps closer and pointed the knife at me. "You should not speak to me that way."

"I'll speak to you however I want. I made you. You wouldn't exist without me."

He laughed. "You didn't make me. I was made in the image of The Huntsman…"

"Right," I said. "And that's all you are, a copy. He was a pathetic weakling who got off on murdering teenage girls. But, you're even less than he was. You're a pale imitation. You're a cover band. And you wouldn't even be that if it wasn't for me. Did you devote your life to imitating the man who tried to kill me? You want to finish his work? And then what? You are what you are because of me. Because I survived. You're nothing without me."

"I'm already nothing," he said. "I was born in November of 1990. The Huntsman's spirit lives on in me. I am a vessel. I was born to complete what he could not. And when I kill you, my life's work will be complete. It doesn't matter what happens to me after that."

"My god," I said, shaking my head. "You really have devoted your entire life to emulating him, haven't you?"

It made me genuinely sad to think about what kind of life he must have had to be obsessed with murders that happened before he was born and to think that he existed to finish them. To think that his reason for living was to kill someone he had never met.

"I feel so sorry for you," I said.

"No," he shook his head emphatically. "You don't get to feel sorry for me. I'm fulfilling my purpose on earth. That is glorious and honorable. You're going to die alone in the woods." He started to close the distance between us. I held out my hand in front of me and he stopped.

He stopped because I was holding a short barrel Smith & Wesson .38 and pointing it at him. His mouth dropped open at the sight of the piece of metal in my hand. This puzzle piece that he couldn't make fit into the scenario that he had planned out.

"I feel sorry for you, because you've devoted your life to copying a sadistic, murdering scumbag. And because you're going to fail."

I pulled the trigger and the sound, even though I knew it was coming, was jarringly loud. It echoed off along the sloping hills on either side of us. The bullet hit him in the stomach and he stumbled and collapsed to the ground. He dropped the knife in front of him, and I hobbled over and kicked it away into the brush. He rolled over onto his side, clutching his stomach as blood trickled through his fingers. He made a few little whimpering sounds. The look on his face was pain mixed with confusion. This wasn't how it was supposed to go.

"What?" I said. "Did you think I was just going to sit here and wait for you to come kill me?"

I've had that gun for almost thirty years. It was my graduation present from my hillbilly uncle, Clyde. He came and visited me in the hospital a few times, and I enjoyed his visits. He was always cheerful, and he was the only one who didn't cry at my bedside and give me hollow reassurances that everything would be all right. To Clyde, I might as well have been there to get my appendix out. He'd sit and tell me corny jokes and tell me he was proud of the way I had handled myself. And when they let me come home, Clyde stopped by to visit and said he had something for me. Gave me the gun and told me it was to protect myself in college. "So's the next one don't put up as much of a fight" and he gave me a wink. I didn't ask him where he got it- he would have just said, "At the gettin' place." And anyway I knew that guys like him, they don't go out and buy guns. They just pick one out of their collection that they don't use very often.

"This is a .38," he had said. "Good for self defense. It don't kick too bad. But it punches as hard as it needs to."

I had to break it to him that I wouldn't be able to take it with me to college. It wouldn't be allowed in "Commiefornia" as he insisted on calling it. He said he would hold on to it for me until I graduated. I didn't expect to ever see it again. But, sure enough, when I came home to visit after graduation, he had it waiting for me. Cleaned, oiled and sighted in. I had only ever used it once before, when I lived in Portland. I was trying to encourage an aggressive junkie to leave my room and politeness wasn't working. I had never fired it before, but I kept it and I always had a feeling that I would need it someday.

I sat back down on the blanket, keeping the gun pointed at him. He was taking deep wheezing breaths, but he was trying to speak.

"I can't believe you did this to me," he said.

"Yeah, I'm sure you can't. I'm sure you expected me to just die like a good little girl. I'm sure it never occurred to you that I was anything but a victim. It takes all the fun out of it when they fight back, doesn't it?"

———————

I pulled my sleeve out of Elise's hand. Gently. I didn't yank it away. And I looked at her and I hope that in that look she knew what I was thinking and felt what I was feeling. That we couldn't keep running. That we would just run and run until the last of our strength bled out of us and then he would take his time in killing us.

I've read that when a rabbit is chased by a predator, sometimes it won't stop running until its heart explodes. I knew I would rather die fighting than run myself to death. I hoped that Elise felt the same way. She just looked at me and there wasn't fear or even confusion on her face. She just looked tired. I led her around the corner and pushed her back against the wall, and she slid down and sat on the floor. I looked at her and tried to make her hear my thoughts. Stay here, please stay here. Her head wobbled, and her eyes looked through me. I didn't want to leave her, but staying there wasn't an option. I ran my hand along her cheek and kissed her forehead. Her skin was so cold. I walked back around the corner. He was still there, still mesmerized by the faces of his victims.

Before I had time to talk myself out of it, I ran. With what little strength I still had left, I ran straight for The Huntsman, lowered my shoulder and drove all of my 145 pounds into the middle of his back. Oh, if the boys on the football team could have seen me. I was much smaller than him, but anyone being hit from behind when they aren't expecting it will get knocked off balance. He pitched forward and collapsed face first through the display case, and the plate glass exploded around him. Shards fell around us like freezing rain. The collision knocked me backward, and I sat down hard on the cement floor. Pain shot through my shoulder and my spine and I was surprised that I was capable of feeling new pain on top of what I already felt.

The Huntsman was kneeling in the display case, like he was praying to the images of the girls he had killed. I heard a strange noise, like the noise little kids make when they're trying not to cry but the sobs force their way through. It was him. He stood up and turned toward me, holding his right wrist in his hand. He must have put his hands out when he fell and they must have gone right through one of the glass shelves. There was a shard of glass several inches long sticking out of the palm of his hand. I could make out his face for the first time, and he was looking at his hand in disbelief. I couldn't keep myself from laughing a little.

While he pulled the shard out of his hand, I got up to my feet. For the first time, I realized how badly injured my knee was. When I put weight on it, there was a sharp pain and the sinking feeling that it would give out and I would fall. I would become very familiar with this sensation in the years to come, but at the time, it was new. I was beyond caring about things like that, though. The pain was meaningless. The only part that bothered me was the possibility of falling and not being able to do what I had to do. He got to his feet, and the knife was in his hand again. I could see the blood oozing around the handle and dripping to the floor. He pushed the hood back from his face.

I saw him clearly for the first time and I recognized him. Not anyone I knew, not really. But, he was familiar. Someone I had seen at the grocery store or on the sidelines at football games. The realization repulsed me. The realization that someone I had spoken to, maybe someone I waved to when we passed on the road, had a secret life where he kept human hearts in jars on his shelf. Thin streams of blood ran down his face. Good, I thought, I hurt you. It wasn't much, but it was a start.

He started walking towards me, slowly now. He wasn't the lunging predator anymore. Or maybe he was waiting for me to turn and run the other way. The fact that I stood my ground seemed to throw him off. He didn't know what I was going to do. I didn't even know what I was going to do.

"I'm gonna gut you, you little bitch. And then I'm gonna find that other little bitch and gut her too." He laughed a little. "I think I like it better this way. Leaving your bodies here for the teachers to find in the morning."

His voice was thin and nasally. It sounded more like a petulant complaint than a threat. In that moment, I couldn't believe I had ever been afraid of him.

Step by step, he came closer. I felt something in me I had never felt before. A seething rage that made me tremble. I had never felt the desire to tear another human being apart with my bare hands before. I wanted to rip his throat out with my teeth. I lunged. I still didn't have a plan. All I knew was that I wanted violence. I wanted to hurt him. If I had to do it bare-handed, so be it. If I had to die in the process, I would take him with me. They would find us the next morning, entwined like lovers, bathing in each other's gore.

When I was a few feet away from him, my feet crunched on the broken glass and, without consciously thinking about what I was doing, I reached down and grabbed a shard. I clenched it in my fist and felt it slice into my fingers. I closed the last few feet between us and I drove the shard into his face. It sliced my fingers down to the bone. But it lodged in his eye and he shrieked. Blood spurted from the socket, and a few drops landed on my face. He swung his hand toward me and I thought for a second that he had punched me in the stomach. I folded in half and tumbled backward onto the floor.

Then my entire midsection exploded in dull, throbbing pain. He hadn't punched me. He had driven the knife into my gut. Blood poured down my legs. I was surprised there was any more left in me. I screamed. I howled. Pain and rage and despair tore out of me until I thought my throat would rip in half. I held my stomach. Oh god, I thought, my guts are going to spill out on to the floor. The blood oozed through my fingers. I sat up. The Huntsman was holding his hand over his eye and blood ran down his cheek. That made me feel a little better. Still, I felt defeated. That he had won. That I was going to die there. That I should have just let him kill me in the house and spared myself the last two hours of running and pain.

Then I saw the knife. There on the floor, between us. Laying in a pile of broken glass, sticky and red. It was closer to me than it was to him. I pulled myself to my feet to go toward it. He started toward the knife, too. I took a step and my knee gave out just enough to make me stagger and draw in a hiss of pain. He stopped, and it registered to him that my knee was injured. He smiled wide like a kid with a new plaything. He closed the short distance between us and before I knew what he was doing, he drove his foot into the side of my knee. My leg folded, and I went down like a sack of cement. The pain took my breath away and made my eyes water.

He started for the knife again. My vision was blurred and I could barely see him. I tried to force my mind to focus on something other than pain. He was almost to the knife, but just then a bell started ringing, loud and persistent. It startled him, and he hesitated. It barely registered for me. A bell ringing was trivial to me at that point. And besides, I had heard it once a month for the last twelve years. Just another fire drill. I lunged forward with the last ounce of strength I had in my one good leg and somehow I made it to the knife before him. I closed my hand around it.

Then the sprinklers went off. Stagnant, black, foul-smelling water cascaded onto us. My hair was plastered to my face. A bloody waterfall cascaded off of me and pooled on the floor. I held the knife out in front of me.

"Don't touch that!" he shrieked again, and now his voice was the petulant cry of a spoiled child who doesn't want to share his toys. "You can't touch that! You're... unclean!"

I rose up and put all of my weight on my right leg. Even straightening out my left leg was so painful I wanted to curl up in a ball and cry. But, somehow- whether adrenaline or endorphins or just blinding rage- I stood and saw him clearly.

"What did you call me?" I gripped the handle tighter. "I'm unclean? Is that what you said, you fucker? I'm unclean?"

This man, this monster who had been wrist-deep in human chest cavities and carried still-warm hearts in his hand. In some way, him calling me unclean was worse than anything he had done to me. I ran at him, in a burst, leading with the knife and I drove it as far as I could into his throat. I've never heard a stuck pig squeal, but I have heard piglets screaming when they are picked up by their hind legs. And that's what he sounded like. He squealed like a piglet being weaned from its mother. I pulled the knife back. Blood poured from his throat and out of his mouth. He looked at me and there was still contempt in his eyes. I drove the knife into him again. Into his chest. Into his heart. To make sure he died.

I've never written about that before. Never told anyone. I lied to the police later. I told them I only stabbed him once and only because he was right on top of me. I'm sure they knew I was lying. They had to have counted the wounds. But no way in hell would a bunch of good old boy, small town Southern police officers question what I did under the circumstances. They were probably happy I saved them the trouble. I watched the life drain out of his eyes. It felt good. He was dead. No doubt about it, no surprise ending where the killer comes back to life. I made sure. He lay on his back with his eyes and mouth open, and the sprinkler water began to fill them up.

I walked, staggered back around the corner to find Elise. She was slumped there on the floor where I had left her. I noticed the fire alarm on the wall above her. She must have gathered up enough strength to pull herself up and yank the handle down at just the right moment. I collapsed onto the floor beside her and wrapped my arms around her. She was shockingly cold, but she was still breathing shallowly.

"You did it sweetie," I said. "You saved me. Again."

I don't know if she could hear me. Her voice was a murmur and I couldn't make out anything she said. I held her, and I rocked her back and forth and I thought that maybe I could hold her in. Keep her inside her body. But I couldn't. I felt her leave. I felt her spirit leave her body, and I felt her go limp. I had a few last minutes with her, but I'm not writing about that. You don't get to know any more about that.

When she was gone, I felt more alone than I had ever felt in my life. I sat holding her and waiting to follow her. I felt sure that I would die any moment, but somehow I didn't. I was left there without her. And I've felt her absence ever since.

After a while, I heard the fire trucks in the distance.

———

"I'll have my revenge. I will kill you for this." He was lying on his side in the dirt and pine needles of the forest floor. Blood soaking the ground around him. He still wouldn't shut up, though.

"No," I said. "You won't." I was sitting on the blanket, cross-legged. I had the gun pointed at him, but casually. He didn't have much fight left in him and what little strength he had left he was using to run his mouth. "You won't get revenge, because in order to have revenge you have to have been wronged. You haven't been wronged. You've gotten exactly what you deserve. You brought all of this on yourself. Plus, you'll never get out of prison. And lastly, if I thought for one second that you would some day come back for me, I'd shoot you in the head right now. So, the more you talk, the more you convince me that maybe I should just kill you. Just to be safe. So, it's probably best if you just shut up and lay there and wait for the cops to get here."

"What makes you think the cops are coming?"

"Well," I said. "I know they're coming. Because I called one of them this morning and left him a voicemail, telling him exactly where I would be. And that you would be here with me, waiting to be arrested."

"What would you have done if I didn't come here?"

"I knew you would come. I called you to me."

"No," he said. "I waited outside your house and I followed you."

"You did exactly what I wanted you to. I don't feel like explaining it to you, and you wouldn't understand, anyway. Tell you what, talking to you is starting to give me a headache. So, if you open your mouth again, I'll put a bullet in it. Okay?"

He didn't respond. The quiet was nice. After a while I heard car tires on the gravel road and then an engine turn off. A door slam. Footsteps on the path to the clearing.

I called out. "Conley?"

"Cassandra? Are you okay?"

"Yes. I'm just a few feet in front of you. There's a clearing. Your suspect is here with me. I have a gun."

"Okay," he said. "When I come into the clearing, make sure your hands are where I can see them."

A moment later he came out of the brush holding a shotgun. He aimed it at the figure on the ground.

"Don't worry," I said. "He's incapacitated."

"I've got him covered. Lay the gun down and then walk around behind me." I did as he said.

Later on, after the radios and the backup from the Sheriff's Department and the ambulance for the suspect and all the questions- I was sitting in the front seat of my little Subaru. Waiting to see what happened next. Conley came over and knelt down by my window.

"Remind me never to piss you off," he said.

"Okay, I'll remind you."

"We didn't find any identification on him. Do you know who he is?"

"No. And I don't care. Did you send someone to tell Anthony what's going on?"

"Yeah, one of the Deputies went over there."

"Am I being detained?"

He shook his head. "I don't see any reason for that. There will be an investigation, of course. I don't see it being anything but self-defense though. The fact that our guy wouldn't stop yelling about how he was going to kill you like all the others, even when they were taking him to the hospital, certainly helps your case. We'll have to hold on to the gun for a while. Which brings me to the part I don't get."

"What's that?"

"You always bring a gun with you when you go out to meditate in the woods?"

"If you're going to ask me questions like that I should call my lawyer."

"This is all off the record. I'm just curious how all of this went down."

"I was waiting for him," I said. I watched to see how he would react to that.

"How did you know he would come here after you? Not ambush you in your house?"

"I warded him away from my home. And I directed him here." He gave me a blank look. "Ask your wife. She'll explain it to you."

"Okay," he said. "Well, you're free to go."

I nodded. "I'm going to stay here for a little longer."

"Calm your nerves?"

"No, I'm calm. I just need some time to figure out how I'm going to write about all this."

# TRACK 13: DISINTEGRATION

At home now and it's getting dark out. Anthony left after I finally convinced him I was in no danger. And that he should go home and get some rest, so he'd be ready when the next psycho starts sending me fan mail. Just me and Jonas, sleeping on the couch beside me, breathing softly. The wind picking up outside playing music with the branches and the wind chimes.

I hadn't thought about that night in years. Except that I never think of anything else. I think back to that roadside, when we gave up on the car and started walking into the darkness. What if I could go back and live in that moment forever? That cold, muddy, bottle-strewn ditch with a million stars in the clear sky overhead. Just stay there for eternity. A kind of purgatory, yes, but my friends would still be there. Still alive. Walking forever. If we never went inside that house, would that night have gone on forever? But if I could do that, go back there and say no, just keep walking. Would I have the right to damn them to that eternity? I would damn myself, happily. Give up everything that came after to live forever in that cold darkness with my friends.

I can't though. I can only write, only evoke them. Conjure

them with words. Once upon a time there was a boy and a girl. Call them back to me. And beg them to forgive me for living.

If only we hadn't gone to the concert, hadn't stopped at the cemetery, hadn't stalled the car, hadn't given up on the car, hadn't gone to that house. They might still be alive. But then he might still be alive too. Might have lived to kill how many more? On and on it goes. This happened because that happened and that happened and that happened.

And it all comes back around and we're back in that car, driving down the road, listening to music. And maybe somewhere we still are, driving forever. And maybe somewhere Joey and Elise are waiting for me. Waiting for me to follow them into the darkness. Until then, I'll just go on and carry their memories inside me.

End.

Thanks for reading!

For a free bonus chapter and news about upcoming books go to:
   https://davidblackwoodbooks.com/mailing-list/
   And sign up!

To hear the playlist go to:

https://davidblackwoodbooks.com/playlists/

If you enjoyed this book, please consider leaving a review!

# ACKNOWLEDGMENTS

First of all, I must apologize to the great Joe R. Lansdale for shamelessly ripping off the title of the prelude from him.

And I must humbly acknowledge the bands whose music inspired this book: Peter Murphy and Bauhaus. Danzig. Nick Cave and The Birthday Party. The Cure. Echo and The Bunnymen. Siouxsie and The Banshees. The Sisters of Mercy. Screams For Tina. Oingo Boingo. The Smiths. Concrete Blonde. Samhain. Christian Death.

I'd also like to thank the absolutely horrible customers at my day job for motivating me to get serious about writing.

And Matthew Revert for making this thing look good.

And Kristina from Truborn Design for making it look good, but different.

And Briana Morgan for her kind encouragement.

And most of all Rachel for finding typos, teaching me about witchcraft, being an awesome mom to our dumb cats, and for taking me seriously when I said I wanted to be a writer.

# ABOUT THE AUTHOR

David Blackwood was born in Akron, Ohio just after Elvis died, but before Lynyrd Skynyrd's plane crashed. On Halloween of that year his family moved to the Shenandoah Valley of Virginia where he lived for the next thirty years. He then spent a year in California before moving to Oregon for the weather.

He has worked as a plumber's laborer, did telemarketing for almost three entire weeks, loaded trucks in a warehouse, worked nights at a motel, sold frozen food out of a truck, counted money in a casino, and repaired slot machines. He considers it a minor miracle that he has never worked in fast food.

David and his wife Rachel live in the coastal forest of Oregon with a bunch of cats and a dog. David's favorite pastimes are reading, listening to music, hoarding physical media, cooking, avoiding social interaction, walking in the woods, and sleeping.

This is David's first book, but there's a real good chance there will be more.